PEGASUS:

A JOURNEY TO NEW EDEN

Thanks to Athina Paris, Editor for your dedication and tireless effort.
Author's photos by Ashography

Revised 02/28/2020
Published By

RockHill Publishing LLC
PO Box 62241
Virginia Beach, VA 23466-2241
www.rockhillpublishing.com

PEGASUS:

A JOURNEY TO NEW EDEN

by

JAMES L HILL

Are you ready for Pegasus ? Are you still pursuing it or.... Overall, this novel is Fantastic!

Disclaimer: I was given an advance review copy by the author. This review is unbiased and only in my honest opinion.

I like the way James described how space, the ship, Pegasus, the trip to Eden so vividly. The whole plot is well-structured and written. Although there some tense moments such as explosion scenes, disagreements, loss, and fighting for survival. The plot is simple to follow, and the writing style is so easy to understand. There are situations that caught me by surprises. I really like what I have read of this novel.

To me, this novel is best for readers that are seeking some sci-fi escapes, colony civilization building, love, compassionate, and some actions to it. Although this novel is a sci-fi action thriller, I believe most women would like to read as the female character, Zuri is a strong woman with a sense of direction and independence. If you like what I have said, you will surely get lots of entertainment and enjoyment out of this novel.

Five Stars – John Black

****

First of all, I'm impressed with the plot. Re-imagining the essence of Noah's Ark with your own twist is brilliant. The notion that companies became more powerful in the future, the United States of Africa, the futuristic science of the Space Spiders and the space colonies – just to name a few – are very well-thought and brilliant. In brief, the world-building of this book is one of the best I've read this year. I'm particularly impressed with the Forest Deck technology and the Westpac project. Dialogue is sharp so as the characterization.

Five Stars – Lit Amri for Readers' Favorite

TO NICKIE, JOHNNY, AL, KENNY, AND JAMES

AND IF YOU FEEL THAT YOU CAN'T GO ON.

AND YOUR WILL'S SINKIN' LOW

JUST BELIEVE AND YOU CAN'T GO WRONG.

IN THE LIGHT YOU WILL FIND THE ROAD.

YOU WILL FIND THE ROAD.

Led Zeppelin

PROLOGUE

War. The one field man excels at. And in the Twentieth Century, we surpassed every expectation with our nature's inherent cruelty. There was The Great War, then the War to End All Wars, followed by fifty years of Cold War. They had to be renamed to World War I and World War II thanks to the Korean War, Vietnam War—not really a war—some called it the Vietnam Conflict, during which 1,353,000 people died. The Soviet-Afghan War, or as the Americans dubbed it, Russia's Vietnam, claimed 2,000,000 souls. Then there were the so-called social wars, the War on Drugs, Ethnic Cleansing, and many, many civil wars. And Africa was especially active in the business of government reorganizations, with social depopulations through decades of ethnic, religious, and tribal conflicts fueled by an ever-increasing supply of better weaponry.

Why war? It was good for business. And to stay in business one needed a product that was in demand and renewable. Regardless of the underlying causes, war fed itself. There was always a need for bigger, better weapons, and people to fight.

It was not disputed that war had pushed technology to new heights. From the years of conflicts during WWI and WWII to the speed and decisiveness of the Six Day War, technology grew by leaps and bounds, and furthered the causes of war.

Likewise, man used the platform of war to unlock the secrets of nature. In less than fifty years we went from discovering the atom to unleashing its power upon the world in its most destructive way. And when we controlled and tamed that power, it was for running our war machines far into the future. We used it to power cities, for that is the basic nature of technology, but technology had a double, for a twin was born out of every discovery, which could be used for good or evil.

Technology took longer to show its benefits to mankind, but it was not technology' fault. Rockets were first developed in the twelfth century, and for eight hundred years, their only use was to put men in graves. But in the latter half of the twentieth century, it put a man on the Moon, and thus, sparked a new age. A technological revolution was born, the Space Age had begun. Once again, technology took a giant leap forward, as it had done from stone to steel and from sail to steam.

An idea was hatched that sounded benign; it was the spirit of man that corrupted that which was good. Communication was the great benefit of the space race. Satellites shrunk the Earth. Instantaneously, we knew what was happening everywhere else around the globe. We knew what conditions were like on worlds we only guessed at before. For the first time, we could pinpoint our exact location in space and time. And that knowledge was quickly turned against us.

Some argued that it was for the better. Because instead of bombing and destroying entire cities, a laser-guided smart bomb eradicated a single target. Drones struck with surgical precision to cut out an enemy in a car on a street, or a room in building, or a building in a city. Such accuracy replaced the need for a fleet of aircraft, or a platoon of soldiers. Technology recreated war, redefined the benefits of power in the hands of a few. With the right weapons and the heart to use them, the few could challenge the many and once more reshape the face of the world and the purpose of mankind.

Man, technology, and war formed a triad of death which none could escape. We had come as far as we could. We stood on the razor edge. Y2K was upon us. The Gulf War would consume us, the Antichrist had risen and the Holy

War begun. The world was overpopulated, its resources dwindling, the environment reeling from centuries of abuse. So many had counted on this, marked their calendars, the twentieth century was surely the end.

Political, religious, and social conflicts sparked immediate responses all over the world. And in a heart-beat, the fires of war flamed up from the smallest, dimmest embers. The same old battles that were fought for centuries were given a new ominous light. Every action viewed in the glow of the doomsday clock. That clock ticked down to the end of 1999. The end of the world was at hand. Everyone held their breath and waited for the finale to be played.

And then the year 2000 was here. We were all still here. Life went on. Welcome to the Twenty-first Century.

CHAPTER ONE

The start of another twelve-hour work day was nothing to look forward to, Zack thought.

'Welcome to the Twenty-first Century' the old sign on the work station greeted him, as usual, and the shuttle ride from the U.S.I Colony 5 was as quiet and boring as always.

As he passed by the U.S. Space Defense Station, he ruminated, "what a waste of time. An hour in flight, another half to suit-up, and now they have me doing antennae work. Nearly ten hours of checking circuits… something a computer can easily do in one."

But as far as the Company was concerned, his time was cheaper than computer time. After all, they did not pay him. At least he would see Zuri on this trip, as she was working a split; one of the beauties of being a free worker, none of the straight twelve-hour work days. Zack almost envied her position with the Company, because although her ties were nearly the same as his, the Company did not own her, as it did him for the next seven years.

"Welcome to the Twenty-First Century, what a joke."

All the hopes and dreams of Utopia people had had, evaded them still, some fifty years past its start. People had traded their freedom, religion, and self-esteem for the promise of a bright and glorious future. But now, instead, that future was like looking at the sun through black glass. Not as bright as one would want, and if you stood looking long enough you would surely go blind. Zack had already gone blind to his situation. All that mattered now was marrying Zuri, and settling the colony.

'*And why not,*' he thought, '*that means freedom, the end of my contract with United Space Industries.*'

The Company was the biggest and the best, and if anyone could start a colony around another star, they could. Also, ten years of room and board was better than any other company was offering. He signed up, also knowing ten years would be impossible to endure, if not for Zuri. In retrospect, five years distance from Earth was not nearly far enough, but he settled for it anyway.

United Space Industries was the first to conquer space. They saw the endless void as a place to grow unchecked; and still unhampered by political constraints, they redefined the meaning of automation the way information had been redefined by the computer. That new definition was the Space Spider, and as their name implied, they spun webs in space.

The body consisted of a laser fusion reactor connected to appendages that secreted crystal steel frames, or poly-plastic streams that they wrapped the framework in, forming great cocoons. Additionally, space spiders could synthesize compounds in various states. One spider, for example, could lay a conduit and the wires that filled it. And they were fast, incredibly so, thanks to electromagnetic propulsion.

Mag-pulsars were volleyball-style spheres filled with liquid nitrogen and a super conductor core. The hexagons comprising the outer shell, were composed of electromagnetics that could be toggled on and off and their strength varied, dotting the spider's body, some large, some small, to drive the spiders in any direction. Every spider had two gigantic mag-pulsars, one on top and one on the belly, but they didn't drive the spider, their job was to create the enormous pressure inside the fusion chamber that produced temperatures as hot as the surface of the sun.

On Earth, maglev-made cars and trains travelled at bullet speeds, in space, the spiders were a hundred times faster. Speed was a necessity, as the materials they extruded solidified instantly in the cold darkness of space.

Always on the pioneering front, U.S.I. developed breeder spiders, which were sent to the asteroid belt. There, they used the plentiful materials to build other huge spiders; the kind they needed to manufacture metropolises. To U.S.I., bigger was best in the void. The Company topped the Fortune 500 with their Space Spider in 2023, before Zack was born. They had been growing unabated ever since.

Zack knew why. Business had a much simpler language than politics, religion, or even science. To a company like U.S.I., there were only debits and credits. U.S.I. took jobs that increased profits and eliminated unnecessary losses.

The United States struck the first deal. During debates over death sentence for terrorists, Congress tried to side-step the issue by granting U.S.I. permission to build U.S. Penal Colony I. The colony was a giant cocoon type, designed to hold a hundred thousand Lifers.

It was run entirely by robots and monitored from Earth stations. It was a hot issue, which only got hotter. Originally, only terrorist, hijackers, or repeat serious felons were supposed to be imprisoned there, but as riots flared up in the early decades, the distinction faded. More and more people were banished to the colonies a hundred thousand miles out in space.

The prisoners were on their own once processed. The colony was totally self-sufficient; solar panels provided energy and farming decks provided food. Even if prisoners didn't work the farms themselves, robots and automated systems kept them producing ample supplies of nourishment. The joke shared by the inmates was, "it's a Garden of Eden in the middle of Hell."

It was strictly survival of the fittest for as long as possible. There were two regulations on Penal Colony I; nobody was allowed on the robotic maintenance levels, and second, everybody had to be in their cells at lights out. To make sure these rules were followed, a transducer was implanted in each prisoner's brain during processing. These made it possible to monitor everyone's whereabouts, and to deliver disciplining electric shocks to defiant inmates. The shock was nonlethal but intolerable, as it could be administered repeatedly without damage to the brain. There was no way to build tolerance, and thus, the unbearable punishment kept even the most hardened criminals out of the restricted zones and in their cells by lights out.

By the year 2040, the penal colonies had grown to sixteen of various sizes. The nations of the U.S.A., the reformed U.S.S.R., South Africa, and Brazil ostracized people by the thousands. There was always room, life span in the colonies ranged from one week to perhaps three years. If you were lucky.

Peter, Zack's oldest brother, had been sent to Penal 3 in 2047, during the Boston Hunger Strike. As the first son of a Black Baptist Minister, he carried a particularly heavy cross. He was expected to be an example, both in his father's eyes and the eyes of a corrupt government.

The economic picture at that time was chaotic. There was a miniscule powerful rich class that controlled companies, countries, and the colonies, then, there was the rest of humanity. Eight and a half billion living on the verge of poverty; starving, homeless, and uneducated, they had little hope. The Earth was turning into a brooder for workers, whom, most companies had little need of, or use for. Automation had replaced the need for humans in all but the most menial jobs. Even the most sophisticated tasks, such as surgeries, could be performed by robots more proficiently.

Peter operated against these ends with demonstrations, sit-ins of government and corporate offices, and political rallies. He was the type of man the country needed; big, bold, and brave enough to say what was wrong with the system, also honest, heartwarming, and highly-educated to know what actions needed to be taken to set things right. Overly charismatic and charming, he became a threat.

At the upcoming Boston Hunger Strike, in Liberty Park, he intended to announce his candidacy for President, but his group was infiltrated by paid agitators. During the fourth night, a rock-throwing mob stormed the police lines and Boston exploded into a blazing city of terror for the next three days. Peter and other leaders of the Baptist Reformers Party were held responsible for the riots, and were summarily tried, convicted, and sentenced. Only Peter was sent to a penal colony. That ended his political career, as well as his life.

At the same time, U.S.I. was busy building factories above the earth. Pharmaceutical companies were among the first to charter a working society and Medical researchers got permission from their governments to sign people up for life studies. Individuals with deadly diseases such as HIV/AIDS, MARV, and Ebola, gave up their freedom for the possibility of a cure.

Unsurprisingly, the United Nations' General Assembly signed a resolution on January 1, 2050, that made any space station operated outside of a fifty-thousand-mile earth limit, autonomous. Thus, making companies, including U.S.I., nations in their own right. More and more, companies made the billion dollar investments for absolute control over their employees.

Most, offering a fifteen-year plan; work the years for room and board then become a full citizen of the colony. But what it meant to be a full citizen of a colony depended entirely on the company that owned it. Usually, it didn't mean much, a mere token vote, and simply room and board for life.

Other companies traded goods for a country's populace. A practice mostly employed by the agricultural stations. A government would send fifty thousand people to work in the fields of a colony in return for a share of its produce. Crops could be planted and grown by automated means, but the best way to harvest was still by backbreaking manual labor. Mainly, the Asian and African nations managed to solve their hunger problems in this manner. U.S.I. had opened a can of worms, but everyone was going fishing with the bait.

I dreaded the start of another twelve-hour shift, but we were coming to the end of phase two at last. Our shuttle turned left, bringing the workstation into full view.

"Welcome to the twenty-first century, from United Space Industries," I said with an acid tone.

"There you go again, Zack. Do you have to read that blasted logo every single trip out?" Arlene was pulling out some silver dollar coins, which she angrily handed over to Bob Marshall.

"Don't mind her, Kid," he said, "you keep it up if you like. You know how some people get when the assignment is nearly over."

"Not really," I said, feeling a little uncomfortable, "this is my first job. And I doubt I ever will, you know I'm shipping out on the Pegasus."

"I wouldn't bet on that, Mr. Tops, you don't know the company execs," Arlene snarled. She was bitter over losing her bet, but her words carried some truth. The

Company has been known to break contracts with their indentures.

"Let's can that kind of chatter," ordered our crew chief, Chilton.

"Yeah, Zack has only been with the company three years, he doesn't know about all the double-crosses yet," added Bob Marshall with just a touch of sarcasm in his gravel voice. His stone-white hair, sandpaper face, and steel blue eyes made him look immortal rather than aged. He had been with the company a long time, much longer than crew chief Chilton. "Yeah, you probably got one of those notarized indentures from the Colonial Regulatory Committee," he continued, smiling at me.

I did, and nodded.

"I hate to tell you that ain't worth shit! If United Space Industries says you go work elsewhere, you go elsewhere. And the Committee, they can go to hell."

"Hey! I said to trash that line," Chilton yelled at him.

"Trash this!" Bob gave him the finger. "I was on my first project, huh… twenty-two years ago now; we were working behind the spiders on U.S. Penal One, Kid."

I assumed he was still talking to me, although he calls everyone Kid. He was strolling the aisle of the shuttle, warming up for another great adventure in the life of Bob Marshall.

"See what you started?" Arlene whispered, "now he'll go on for the whole hour, 'til we dock at the station."

I shrugged and pretended to be bored also. But actually, this would be the best part of the shift. Well, second best, I planned to meet Zuri for lunch aboard Pegasus later, and I was going to make sure I reached Deck 17 by lunchtime.

"Like I was saying, Kid," Bob's gaunt six-one frame towered over me. "They were supposed to shut down the space spiders while we inspected the framework and if I had not seen its shadow on the beam below I would have been caught like the rest. I jumped from the beam just in time. As I bounced around on my tether line I watched the others get sprayed with aluminized iron silicate. Sixteen of them encased in that stuff, alive. I could hear them frantically calling for help inside their hard-suits. It took hours to cut them out, even with laser torches. Yeah, they ran out of air long before we could free them from the beam. Shit! The Company said the spider had glitched its programming. But I knew better, those bastards never turned the damn thing off. After the spider refilled its tanks, it came back to lay more frame, right where we were standing. The Company never paid death benefits, just like that, wiggled out. They transferred me to the defense station the next day. It was a restricted project so I had no outside contact for four years. U.S.I. swept the whole affair under the carpet."

"That's the way it always is out here," Arlene said. "Robots work and we check. Robots screw up and we die. Nobody regulates a damn thing."

Arlene was a beautiful redheaded Irish woman and when I started at U.S.I., she was my instructor. I thought she was a teenager then, maybe eighteen, but she quickly set the record straight.

"I was indentured by U.S.I. seven years ago, when I was fifteen. Staying for a full twenty."

She had been signed over by the British government, in lieu of doing life in a penal colony for rioting. She didn't talk about it much; after all, a lot of indentures were proffered instead of doing prison time. Any number of governments rounded up its dissenters and gladly sent them off to work for the companies. Those who refused went to places like U.S. Penal One, Interpol's Space Confinement Center, or the Russian Black Star.

I, of course, did not belong to that class of workers. I voluntarily signed up for work on Pegasus and as part of my agreement, was to be among the first to settle another solar system. Zuri and I will be in a colony of seventy-five thousand pioneers.

"Don't think because you are not sentenced they can't change your assignment, now that the work is done," she cautioned me, "I was going to get married once, while I was working on Outworld. All the papers were signed, everything was ready. We even had a unit assigned to us."

"What went wrong?" I found myself asking.

"Nothing went wrong. The dirty bloody buggers back-doored us. They gave him orders to monitor a freaking mole transformer in the asteroid belt. You know the kind, Old-timer; those spiders that bore into an asteroid and suck out its insides to make a freighter hull or something stupid like that. We could still have married," her voice was seething with unvented anger, "but naturally, we would have to live at the mole station. I guess they didn't want any convicts at Outworld. They gave us a right royal bumming."

"He broke off the engagement."

"No," she smiled. "He was a real right guy. I called it off, as I couldn't let him waste ten years of his life in a tomb for me. I'd rather go to a penal colony. At least death would come quickly."

I wanted to say that couldn't happen to me, but I knew it was wiser not to. Because, I have Zuri, who paid her way, and she is down on the contract. I hated having her sign a marriage contract, but it was the only way to guarantee we didn't get screwed. Also, I hate that we have to wait five years to get married. But the contract states we have to be past the no-turn-back point before we can marry.

So, I guess Arlene and Bob are right, the company has two more years to screw me over.

Out of our shuttle window the logo took on its true appearance, black solar panels a mile long on the white aluminized iron silicate walls. The panels provided all the energy the station required. We were nearing a docking bay door in the workstation, which hid the Pegasus from view. The station filled twenty-five cubic miles of space. Pegasus filled most of it.

The workstation was nothing more than a set of pressure chambers and landing docks, and interior lights constantly bathed the ship. It was quiet, even for space, and that was the one thing I could not adjust to these past few weeks, as I had become accustomed to the endless chatter of the radio. The station was a ghost town now, most of the job rooms had been shut down to conserve energy, making the place look like a checkerboard box internally.

I was inside the ready room oiling my suit's O-joints. I can't afford to have this stupid thing locking up on me. The thought of a spider spraying me jumped into my head. I pushed the image out. Part of my training videos were horrific films of people hit by spiders, sprayed by spiders, and lifelines cut by spiders. There was a warning alarm that went off in the helmet when a spider was approaching, but sometimes you just didn't hear it, or foolishly disabled it.

The next time I see Zuri will be mid-way through my shift. I am going to make lunch today. *'So, nothing is going to hold me up, especially not this stupid hard-shell, and definitely not getting killed by a metal monster.'*

I stepped up onto the boots' platform and snapped the leg casings around my lower half. I worked my legs around, they felt good. Next, I donned the upper torso and checked my chest plate indicators, everything was OK, the air blowing soft and cool up my back. Pulling the two thick plates together made the magnets lock. The suits were made so they could be opened from the inside. I slipped my arms through the holes. Once I secured the helmet and gloves I was ready.

"Arlene, where are you?"

"I'm on the A wing. Have a good walkdown."

"I'll be at portside top."

A spider whisked past me as I slid down my tether line. We had to check in with our partner before starting out, as a safety precaution. Switching on my electron scanner, I called in, "Control... Control... Zackary Tops, sector 115T." I started walking down the outer hull, looking for a blip on the scope, one that usually doesn't occur. It is ten hours of loneliness. Ten hours to meditate. It is madness. This has to be the worst duty I ever pulled.

Electronic sweep in hand, the plodding of my footsteps in diligent performance of my duty, and eyes fixed on the meter hoping for a flicker of the lamp, I'm feeling real lost. During these ten hours, I rarely get a blip. Occasionally, a spider will eject from a portal in Pegasus going for a refill. Looking towards the blackened cubicles of the station, I know we are all alone out here.

Time goes by slower and slower as one walks the gangplanks and I have become accustomed to doing the walkdown without a tether line, from watching Bob. He often tells me that he would rather use his air to jet back to safety than a damned tether. Now I know why. I realize I don't know him as well as I think... Or myself. After all, this is your basic slave chain.

"They don't need armies. The weak go willingly." Dad's preacher voice boomed in my helmet.

"What! Who was that?"

"Go back to school, get something for yourself. Stop running, God has big plans for you, boy." Even this far in space, a hundred thousand miles, halfway to the moon, and he still taunts me. This long in time, he tears, accuses, ridicules, mocks, diminishes, and condemns me.

After Peter died, I was supposed to fill his shoes. Take his place in the family business of saving souls and fighting for the little guy. The only problem, I was the little guy, Peter's scrawny little brother. Just one of seven, third of four boys in the family. I had neither Peter's stature nor the voice of God like Dad. Even my three sisters had more going for them than I did. One a lawyer, the other a doctor, and the youngest of us all married a minister. She made dad very proud. Oh, my other problem, I was not sure God had planned on me. On the Eternal List of Angels, Saints, and Martyrs, my name didn't even show up. I bombed out of Seminary School for what was termed, "lack of conviction."

"Was that you, Zack?" Arlene's voice queried from my helmet's speaker.

"Let him be." Bob commanded.

"This is Control. Does anybody want to report?"

"No," I said.

The walkdown continued. I carried the weight of my father's disdain on my shoulders alone.

Sometime later, I picked up a flasher on my scope. Of all the days to pick up a flaw in the webbing, "I've got a glitch for you—quality control guys."

"Marked. Go on correction."

"Marked. Out."

I pulled an egg from my sling pouch. Technically, it's an electric gravity generator; but it looks like an egg, an ostrich egg to be precise, except for the feet. Anyway, I extended the tripods and placed it on the spot, turned its silver dome, and sat down on the torso ring of my suit to wait for a repair spider to answer my signal.

Between the outer hull and the inner hull—both made of aluminized iron silicate crystal—there are layers upon layers of webbing. One inside another spun just right in dimension, so they never touch. The repair spider will dissolve the bad spot and secrete a new one in its place. All I have to do is wait. I tell myself this is important, and it is. If a high-power web is crossed, with say, the antenna webbing, the radioman gets fried. I just happen to be a radioman.

CHAPTER TWO

The shuttle was on its final approach.

Pegasus' globe head sat just inside the workstation's bay. Its large command center was disproportionate to her delicate slim neck and slender body, and her pair of wings rose from the broad flat back in long even rows like an amphitheater. These arms were essentially multiple levels of atomic accelerators, which produced the immense gravitational fields that would propel her. The accelerators flung atomic particles through miles of corridors in the extensions and ultimately into each other in total annihilation, releasing pure energy. Energy that would form the gravity sphere around the entire craft and allow her to slip through space-time. The crew within the massive dome would direct the flow of power surging through the orb, modify its orientation, and thus the destination of the vessel.

Zuri stared at the ship in awe. She had seen her as an embryo of chutes and ladders, watched her grow with white silken skin inching over the frame day by day, but only now did she seem alive. Now that she was solid, her size intimidating, and her presence immense. Pegasus dominated the work station and demanded attention.

The shuttle floated between her wings, heading for the aft shuttle bays. Below, Zuri counted a dozen hard-suits on a walkdown. One person stood transfixed before an egg, reflecting its rhythmic red, yellow, and blue lights. She knew one of those hard-suits held Zack; which one, she did not know.

"*Poor Zack*," Zuri thought. He had walkdown duty for a month and when he finished a day in a hard-suit all he could do was sleep. He was drawn and losing weight. Zack described the work as trying to walk in tomato soup up to one's neck, that was about to boil.

I was going to work in Pegasus' communications center. As a Technical Advisor, I located flaws in the computer's language programming. The computer had to respond to a hundred and eight different languages and translate on demand. With all the nationalities that are involved in this project, communication is a huge headache. In her belly, Pegasus has three halls of language computers alone.

My equipment arrived in the form of a four-foot-tall truck-like robot. I speak into a terminal, the computer translates and transmits the message, and the robot receives it from the output source and compares it for accuracy. The robot can also pick up sounds originating in any part of Pegasus with its sensitive microphones. And for this unnerving ability, we nicknamed it Big Ears.

Language is a strange concept for computers, as a lot of its meaning is tied up in tone. What may be a sound of rejoicing in one culture, can very well be the sound of lamenting to another. The computer must match the intention with the meaning exactly, or a joke becomes an insult.

A quick system check, and things look pretty good from here; now, it is time to get down to the real work. I dispatched my crew: John Dyre to the bridge, Shara Welsch to the medical deck, and Edwin Puma to the reactor deck. When each person reaches their designated area, we will begin our drama. Today, I feel like hearing a little Shakespeare.

Each will read parts in a pre-chosen tongue and I will check the output with Big Ears. I am particularly interested in how the computers will handle Puma's Macbeth. He is a full blooded Shinnecock Indian who speaks a dialect, that in six years of international communications, I have never heard. He told me that his father's fathers passed it down orally. This will be the first time his language has ever been recorded and I feel the extreme importance he placed in having their dialect in Pegasus' memory. But it is ironic that everything else Pegasus stands for, he opposes.

"This project raped the world, and its leaders bastardized the people..."

I know whom he means, the indentured, the imprisoned, and the forgotten.

"We walk with the gods and our envy mocks our every step," Puma says in the quiet times when words hold their greatest truth. Or sometimes he says, "We are prisoners, like the sparrow is a prisoner of the sky."

I'll bet that sounds great in his language.

That is what is wrong with society today, too much talking, no one listening. Not to their people, nor their allies and adversaries, not even themselves. It is like doing Shakespeare in ten languages. Because while governments negotiated, people died. While companies traded, countries starved. The world was choking and our leaders never bothered to take a breath.

Even my father, Mlimo, I am sorry to say, did not hear. In the years after the Fall, he became obsessed with keeping up with the White World.

"We must prove ourselves," he would charge the Senate, "not to those who wait to see us fail, but to our own! The Republic must be strong; our people must have faith in their abilities. Or we will be swallowed up again."

As the Minister of Agriculture, he had the toughest job to perform. His mission was to turn war-ravaged lands into productive healthy fields, and feed the millions that were starving, on a continent that for so long had been abused. As a little girl, I heard him, night after night, debating the problems to the empty air. And during the days, his fervent debates would resonate in the Central Ministry.

"We need to establish the western sectors for herding. And to become self-sufficient, we must build an irrigation system throughout the Southlands."

But other ministers had their own plans for the lands and the masses. Some people wanted nothing to do with the Central Ministry or the United States of Africa. They wanted to return to the lives of their ancestry. They had their fill of governments, but going back was impossible.

It wasn't just European influences that people were trying to expel. That had been easier after the fall of Apartheid in South Africa in the late twentieth century. Which did not end quietly or go away quickly, the South African government had multiple restarts, before finally expelling all nonblack citizens from the country.

The formation of the United States of Africa was an attempt to unify the nations under one banner for the prosperity of all black Africans, to return to pre-colonial days, however, cultural and ancestral divisions dated back millennia. The nations that had riches of gold and other precious minerals, or sufficient farmlands, had no desire to help their ancient enemies. The U.S.A. was in constant turmoil, but it did manage to end a century of civil wars across Africa, and the people finally started moving forward.

By the time I was six-years-old, we had lived in no less than fifty different places. Sometimes, we stayed only a couple of days before boarding another bus to another corner of the continent. I had few friends during my life.

My mother died when I was very young and my father's position kept us moving. I lived in everything, from grass huts, to large communal houses, to palaces. And I always felt out of place.

When the United States of America offered Father a chance to join the extraterrestrial farms, he reluctantly agreed, because for him, it was the chance to end squabbling over land. He demanded and got full partnership between the two U.S.As. Unlike some Asian nations which sent people to the colony, but had no voice in its operations, he arranged for some modules to be built and operated by Africans. The deal was applauded by the other ministers. He had bargained hard with a major world power and thus uplifted the new nation's standing. However, all were not pleased, because to keep his bargain he had to draft workers. No matter what the reasons, some wanted nothing more to do with the White World.

Two days past my eighteenth birthday, while I was studying at the National University of Bangui, I received word that my father was dead. Shot down on his way to the Central Ministry. The Whites had been expelled a decade ago, yet the riots continued. The killing, the tire burning, the villainy spoke so loud, we couldn't hear the people's woes. Ours was a difficult time.

I often wonder what Father would have thought of Zack, because in many ways, they mirror each other. Zackary Tops is a man of strong convictions and even stronger will. We met in Europe at an electronics convention and it was not love at first sight. He was fresh out of the U.S. Army, I didn't like that. The way he spoke of it, which was very little to nearly not at all, I could tell he didn't like it either.

He often lamented, "it was just another job I had to do."

But like Father, he never backed down from a challenge. Father would say, "there is always a solution to be had if you can define the problem at hand."

The team and I finally reached Romeo and Juliet. I am Juliet… and my Romeo is on a walkdown, of course. In just a few hours, we will be joined in a secret meeting, a romantic interlude in the woods. Shakespeare knew love is ageless.

CHAPTER THREE

I made it to Deck 17 at 1200 hours and found Zuri sitting on the grass. The Forest Deck was our favorite place in the ship. The smell of fresh grass and pine in the air, the jays playing and singing songs in the blue sky. This is how Earth should be.

"Zack, baby! This way," called Zuri, "Isn't this just the perfect spot for a picnic? The brook is rolling down the slope so crystal clear. Oh, look! Did you see that fish?"

"Yeah. It's a striped bass. I think. Dad took us fishing for them in the old days."

"The Old Days," she chuckled, "you sound like you're turning into an old man, Zackary Tops. There is so much beauty here… it's truly amazing what people can do when they want to. A thousand acres of New England forest complete with birds, fish, sunshine, and even clouds."

"The sunshine and clouds are artificially produced," I repined.

Truthfully, they were as real as actual trees, birds, and fish. U.S.I. took a slice of Earth and transplanted it whole into Pegasus. They carved many slices straight from the world and gave each a deck. Living, breathing, growing parts of the planet carefully nurtured, even down to authentic sunlight. It was piped throughout the ship via optical cables from her outermost skin. Once we are in deep space, the sunlight will come from our fusion accelerators. At light speed, Pegasus will produce a photosphere as she vents energy through this covering. She will be a true starship.

When I consider this side of the twenty-first century, I am awestruck. The possibilities are unlimited and reality unimaginable. There are decks for every type of life form. Each deck's climate is controlled and held in delicate balance by the environmental computers. It is too bad no one thought it worth the time and effort to do the same on Earth. Governments and corporations neglected and abused the planet for so long life was barely hanging on. Pegasus rescued many endangered species that would otherwise have vanished by now. Complete ecosystems were recreated for transportation to the planet we named, New Eden. Every type of creature was represented on this new Ark.

But it wasn't just fauna and flora Pegasus was meant to preserve. Mostly, couples were signed for the journey. U.S.I. wanted only married or engaged people, but a few families were also going, like the Chief Engineer, Charlie Katz. His kids were teenagers, so he had to receive a special clearance. The project managers wanted to be careful that no one got homesick and wanted to go back. Psychologically speaking, kids and singles exhibited negative tendencies. Those instincts have ruined long-term projects in the past.

But all these concerns seem far away now, because the only thing that matters is us. We are the only people in this world. We eat, drink, and roll in the long grass like kids on holiday.

These are the good moments I cherish, the respites from a strife-riddled life. I hold onto these instants for as long as possible before going back to the others, as we have barely seen each other these days. I so dearly miss the rose-scented braids that curled around her head. I miss the way she crowned herself with delicately interwoven diamond threads. I dream about the way her lips quiver as laughter slips from them.

Now, all I have is an occasional dinner note taped to the food processor, or a short moment between shifts. It is like living with a ghost. I am nothing but a shadow in our unit anyway. My mood-swings come much more frequently these days, probably from the increased stress.

Zuri, with her wide wild eyes, can read my changes like a book. "What troubles you, here in our little love garden?"

"Oh, nothing really," I sighed, "everything is fine. I'm just a little worn out."

"Well, by this time next week, we will be on our way. Behind us will be the sick and demented, before us a promising fresh and new future."

"Can we really get away? They will still own me," I despaired.

"No!" She flared. "They never owned you. It's just a contract, a piece of paper and nothing more. I can't understand how you let yourself think it's anything else."

"Because it is; they control my time, where I go, and when." I was sitting up stiff. Angrily, I threw a stone into the brook. I was angry that I had changed the mood. "I won't be safe until we pass the Martian processing plant. Hell, they can easily reassign me before we reach the Belt. I won't feel safe until we hit hyperspace."

"They can't re-assign you at all; remember, we both signed a contract with U.S.I."

Her words were acid eating through my heart.

She continued sweetly. "It's our guarantee, honey. We both know we need one to deal with them." She pulled me back down next to her.

We stared up at the clouds drifting along on the perpetual breeze. The songs of the birds filled our silence. We lay motionless until my watch alarm signaled lunch was over.

All too soon, I was back in my hard-suit on the outer deck, while Zuri returned to her language computers and robots. Our two crews comprise the entire staff of the workstation. Even security had pulled back to the comfort of Colony 5 because once the gravitational drivers were charged and polarized, it was safer to monitor Pegasus from the colony. An accidental engine start-up would shatter the station, completely pulverize the structure, and turn it into a cloud of dust a hundred miles wide. No particle of man or machine would be left larger than a grain of sand.

They finished the relays in the wings a month ago, so we will be pulling out in a matter of days. The Company is moving very fast, of that I was sure. And the others, Bob and Arlene, felt it too. The constant double-shifting, Zuri's complete run-through of the computer systems; instead of sectional runs. For the last four months, the Company has operated on full burners. But something is not right; we still have a lot of time left in our launch window.

We have a year and a half to cross the Belt and kick in the gravitational drivers. It is close to impossible to traverse the asteroid belt using the drivers without dragging one of them into our magnetic field, and when we cut the power off, the asteroid would come barreling through. Therefore, the plan is to use only laser rockets until then. The powerful beams focus on reflectors deep in the underbelly of Pegasus to propel her forward. With them, we will be beyond the Belt in four months. So, why the big rush? It was beyond me.

I switch my suit's radio to short range. "Bob."

"Yeah, Kid, what's on your mind?"

"We are pulling out next week," I rejoiced.

"You are. I'm not signed up for the fantasy cruise."

"Well, isn't that rather soon?" I knew he's been on a dozen jobs.

"Kid, this is a strictly build'em and ship'em deal," his tone was anything but fatherly or believable. "Yeah, one hour after you guys pull out, we'll be working on another one. Just roll on and happy voyage."

"Are you sure? Zuri—"

"Let me tell you this. Once you're out the door, you are on your own. No guarantees, no warranty. If this ship blows apart two minutes after you are underway, that's your bad luck. The Company has been paid in advance, so your failure will only be a minor setback in designing."

"OK, I know where you're coming from." My mind was at ease once more.

Zuri had heard rumors of a strike or injunction being planned against U.S.I. Her ties in the diplomatic communities give her information not readily known. The company has its spies and bribes plenty to be in the know, but she has respect and that is something that goes much further than money.

Apparently, some countries wanted to halt the Pegasus Project entirely. Because, she had also heard, talk of challenging U.S.I.'s right to take Earth's living resources from the planet. I couldn't imagine on what grounds someone would base such a lawsuit, but they could delay us for years to come, while they fought back and forth.

Bob was to my right on the Top Deck. He gave me a wave.

Zuri was planning to wait for me until the end of my walkdown, then, we would shuttle back together. I quickened my step, hoping as I did that nothing else popped up on this swing.

Since lunch… when was that? It already feels as if I haven't been on Deck 17 in months. I had almost forgotten how green trees can be.

Zuri's favorites are pines, because of the first time she saw trees that stayed green, even during the cold of winter. She had told me when we met in Europe, "Pines are the original life of Earth."

I told her I had read differently. She loves the forest, and so do I. Funny, after leaving Colombia, I never thought I would want to see trees again.

The actual war between the U.S. and Colombia lasted only six hours, but the occupation dragged on for years, the way wars tend do. That was why they reinstated the draft. That was why I had to serve five years. That was why I was in the Colombian jungle. That was why I hated trees.

I don't know exactly what transpired, but it involved a shipload of drugs. The boat was in New York's harbor when it blew up, and it destroyed a large portion of Brooklyn. Both countries blamed the other for the catastrophe. The only thing that matters is that America retaliated with three rocket-launching destroyers. In a six-hour bombardment, they crushed and scattered the Colombian government. Their capital going up in miles of chemical flames. The military splintered into guerrilla bands and about seven years later, my turn came to walk in the woods.

We rode Whisper Raiders, a sort of motorcycle on a wedge. It used a rocket rotary engine to turn its twin turbine fans. It rose knee-high and glided on the compressed air from its bottom turbine. And the rear one kicked like a mule for such a small unit.

The Raiders packed a nasty little arsenal in the wedge. They were equipped with a dozen SNIP's (small nuclear incendiary projectiles) on guided missiles with a hundred-mile range, and four unidirectional machine guns; two antipersonnel and two armor-piercing types.

Most of the force stayed off shore on the carriers. The rehabilitation was being done by some civilian outfits, reconstruction was what they called it. But all they did was put the Colombian Liberatees to work building condominiums. They restored miles of beachfronts to the sleek modern living for the traveling set. The people… well, they were marginally better off than when the drug czars reigned. That is what I kept telling myself.

And as for the guerrillas… I made a sweep every night for three years. When we came upon a campsite in the jungle it was a few minutes of rock and roll on the guns. But sometimes, they were well fortified, dug in the ground with bazookas and anti-aircraft guns. We would have quite a day of it then. We found some rebel groups with air support, mainly ragtag copters, but they did the job. At times, things got real heavy, as when my team of six raiders found a reformed unit.

They were easily three-hundred strong and had dug into the hillsides around Palmira. Our silence and speed was our edge. We hovered fifty-yards from the center of the camp. We attacked what we thought were a few small barracks and a couple of weapon depots. Moments later we knew we had hit a rebel insurgent force.

"Snake Six. Snake Six, this is Snake Two," I blurted out, "it's getting hairy around here. I suggest doing some cross and runs."

We bobbed up and down in the night sky, colors dancing around us. From our maximum altitude of fifty-feet we fired into the enemy's guns' haze.

"Snake Three, you got a smoker on your tail!"

"Got it! Thanks, Five."

As our weapons depleted, we played our last option, a SNIP. We super-sonicked out of there and fired one behind us. The projectile is a six-inch bullet with an atomic core. On impact, the core is exposed and a flashover occurs. Five square miles of jungle was turned into a sea of flames, and then, poof, it was out.

"Man, did you see that! Wow, it's getting hot, ain't it, Snake One."

"Yeah, Kid. Take a swallow now, you are dehydrating."

Wait, what? That's Bob Marshall. Oh, right.

"Hey, Kid, are you still on the line?"

"I'm right here, Bob." I tried to sound normal.

"OK. Don't think because you're shipping out soon, you'll be sailing away. Remember, every garden has its snakes."

"Let's tighten up those lines, boys," Chilton boomed.

"Jesus, Chilton! Are you always a prick?" Marshall's voice thundered inside my helmet. "Can't you see we are getting a little airy? Anyway, Zack, you and that cutie grab all you can get. This adventure is going to be a capitalist's Heaven. Yeah, in this life you keep your eyes to the future. You might be thinking, *why isn't Ol' Bob taking the trip?*"

He was getting into one of his stories. I'm glad, his adventures are usually happy ones.

"Yeah, I'm telling you, I worked for this outfit a lot of years, doing mining. Hell, doing everything. Part of my pay I deferred to resort shares. Not just any resort, mind you, The Golden Galaxy."

I was impressed; The Golden Galaxy is a step away from being an outlawed colony. Their lifestyle, let's say, is not to the Committee's liking, but they do allow the Colonial Guard to land at their own discretion. Plus, they signed an extradition treaty, so the Committee can't ban trade with them. Prostitution, narcotics, and other wanton activities, that can be found nowhere else, are recklessly traded there.

It didn't surprise me that Bob would manage membership at the 'resort'. He wasn't rich but he was resourceful. I also understood why he waited to go there, not many people from the Golden Galaxy are welcome at the other colonies. Everybody goes there under an alias or to stay. His big bearded face suggested he could find happiness no place else than at a modern Barbary Coast.

When Bob spoke of snakes he was usually referring to Franc Swedter, the Mission Executive. His position wasn't quite clear. He ranked somewhere below the Captain and above everyone else. He assigned the work detail and hired the crew. Franc Swedter also drew up the passenger list. Ninety percent of the seventy-five thousand people on Pegasus bought their trip to paradise from him. The price tag was a whooping five hundred thousand American dollars.

For this modest amount, one got to bring a thousand pounds of personal effects, and received one cabin mate to handle their affairs. I have a feeling that after we are on our way, all the indentures will be reduced to servants by Swedter.

Although the ship has a full complement of robots to do domestic chores, human servants are still more desirable. After all, one cannot feel superior to a machine, and that is still the basic need that servants fulfil.

Swedter's basic need took the form of command. Someone told me he had tried for a captain's position with the company. He was turned down twice, before settling for mission executive on Pegasus, but to look at him one would think he was our captain. He dresses in day whites and navy blue at night, always military pressed. I can tell he has some training, but his Dutch accent has kept him from his goal. U.S.I. never promotes foreigners too high up in the company, so he became our despot and the Company's flunky.

More than likely we will bump into each other at tonight's inauguration. Anyway, I really don't have much to worry about from him, because once we are underway, it's possible I will draw light duties. Like all little men in big men shoes, he is too busy licking Zuri's boots to bother me. Being a diplomat's daughter was all it took for him to fall over himself to please her. The added fact that her name, Zuri Mujaji, means: "Beautiful empress rainmaker," makes him an intolerable sham. The sight of his pretentiousness makes me wretch, but she takes it in stride though, pouring on her accent thickly, just as he does his phony one. Hers sounds melodic and sweet while his, makes me want to say, "Come on, you're really from Brooklyn."

I was waiting at Airlock 203.

Puma arrived on a tri-cart and began loading his gear into the shuttle. "So, Zuri, you are staying behind?" He queried.

"Don't worry, Zackary and I will catch a cargo loader back. How did it go in the library?" I asked.

"Well. I didn't have enough time to finish, but I laid down the phonetic structure. I also put down some of our stories."

I wanted to ask if I could go listen to them, but felt uneasy. I will have my chance, but for now, I'll leave him to his privacy. But there was something I was dying to know. "Why didn't you sign on with us? You would have been able to put down all of your people's culture then. They could live on in a new land."

"Is that why you are going, Zuri, to bring your people to a new land?"

"Huh, no, not really," I had offended him. The dim light of the airlock cubical reflected from his red face, reminding me of old western movies. "I'm going to start a different life, for Zackary and me, away from the poverty and slavery that is here."

"I am neither poor nor a slave but my life is coming to an end, therefore, it is not my time to start anew. I am recording my history for you to give to the Great One, so he will not forget us. I left some cubes in the library, the computers are transcribing them. If you are still here when they are done, please end the downloading."

"How will I know if the computer picked them up correctly?"

"Listen to them."

Through the large plastic window of the airlock door, I watched Puma board the Shuttle. His walk was cat-like; feet seeming to barely touch the floor. His sleek frame slipped through places just as his name suggested. He amazed me. But what did he mean when he said his life was near its end? From his general appearance, I would place his age at thirty-five.

I don't know much about the American Indian, merely that the whites almost annihilated their culture in the nineteenth and twentieth centuries. It dawned on me then that I knew next to nothing about Edwin Puma, and it wasn't because he was withdrawn or aloof. In fact, he was just the opposite, cheerful and talkative. Fluency in twenty human and ten computer languages made him very comfortable with people. His capabilities far outshine mine or anybody that I know. Yet, modesty is his greatest virtue and so, this American Indian remains a mystery to me.

While I watched the launch platform quietly push a shuttle out of the bay, I realized he was rarely the subject of his own conversations. The shuttle cleared the workstation before igniting its rockets. It quickly disappeared around the side of the station and I walked over to the control panel just outside the bay.

"Outer view, please," I requested from Pegasus.

The white ceramic wall turned into a ten-foot picture window. I could see some of Zackary's crew sliding up their cables. I took the tri-cart over to Deck 18.

The platform's yellow lights reflected inside the silvery access tube and then the magnetic boots came into view. Thick soles of iron coils six-inches high topped by the sky blue ceramic feet and calves' sections. Silver discs at the knees and thighs passed by until the body and helmet came to a rest behind the airlock window.

The door rose and Zack took a few thunderous steps into the room. Walking with the suit on in zero gravity was difficult, the magnetic boots made it feel like walking on wet tar. But under full gravity, it was impossible to move in a suit that weighed five hundred pounds. The servo-motors at the joints made it barely awkwardly doable.

Zuri pressed the wrist controls and the helmet rose on its vertebra. Then climbing up on my boots, she kissed me playfully.

I pulled off my outer gloves, revealing the black rubber ones of the soft-suit lining. I frowned. "You are not going to like the smell inside this soup can."

"That's why I kissed you now," she laughed.

I unlocked the suit and stepped out in my shorts. My knees looked large and round like the suit's.

"Hey, working in that suit is really making you lose weight." She observed. "I'm going to make sure you get plenty to eat at tonight's ball."

"I wish I could just sleep for the next two days."

"C'mon," she stamped, "it wouldn't be any fun without you."

"You got Puma to come, and Marshall. Hell, that's a party right there! The two of them together on Pegasus…

they'll tear the place up. They might even do enough damage to delay our leaving another two years."

"But they are not you. Anyway, I'm not sure if Puma is coming. We had the oddest conversation a while ago." She had a determined look, which meant, it was time to give up.

We rode down the corridors with my suit plodding behind us. "I have to drop off the suit up on Six, so give me a few, OK?"

"Then you can get a little rest onboard before tonight," Zuri suggested.

"You know they don't like that."

"After next week, we'll be living here, so screw them." She was borrowing one of my pet sayings. Only, when she said it, her voice had a hint of caution. "I have to check on some work he left running anyway. Oh, and I still need to check the V.I.P. communicators."

I woke to the sounds and smells of Zuri's cooking. Some of the living quarters, like ours, have small kitchens. Although they prefer everyone to eat in the dining rooms, to promote unity, the V.I.P.s have a microwave oven, pullout range, and wall refrigerator.

Zuri's dad left her a large legacy; assassination elevated him to the status of Lincoln and Kennedy, turning her into an unwitting and unwilling symbol for unity. Zuri made televised speeches at brotherhood rallies across Africa. They had her on a treadmill for years. She was on a government sponsored trip when we met.

I looked at the night table clock, 1800 hours; we still had a few hours of solitude.

We spoke at length about the tri-star solar system of Alpha Centauri. Ever since the Hubble Space Telescope detected the presence of its seven planets, our single-star solar system seemed boring. People became obsessed with exploring these new worlds, even while most of our own was still unexplored, and most likely would remain so. Only the asteroid belt, Mars, and a few moons of the outer planets were being mined for their resources.

The cost of transforming a planet from a hostile environment to one suitable for life is astronomical, it's far more practical to build space colonies. Most people who decided to live in them adjusted quickly to the artificial world of colonies. Not me, I still needed open spaces, the sky above me, and dirt below. Worst of all were the walls, everywhere, they closed me in. They were something I could never get used to.

After dinner, we went to the Observation Deck in the globe section. We wanted to watch the shuttles arriving. Some of them would be coming directly from Earth, carrying dignitaries to see their people off.

For the last three years, this trip was hawked as "The Greatest Adventure of Mankind." Although we have yet to receive data from the probes that were sent, everyone is sure of success; we expect to be filled in on the way. But it wasn't just the spirit of adventure that drove the project; because if we locate a planet that is inhabitable it will be a lot cheaper than transforming, terraforming, or colony building it. As predicted by many, Earth is beyond saving, and there are countless individuals and organizations with divergent agendas to make it work. So here we stand, looking at it from one hundred thousand miles away, hating her and missing her in the same moment. We watched her in silence.

CHAPTER FOUR

Francois Swedter was in the Control Center on Colony 5 with Pegasus' Captain Brolocci. They were supervising the almost continuous arrivals of guests.

Jump-jets left Earth, one an hour, for the colony. The white and blue U.S.I. craft was the perfect marriage of jumbo jet and rocket ship. It took off and landed like a jet, and in the stratosphere the turbines closed and the three tail engines transformed to rocket engines. Upward they flew for six hours across the fifty thousand miles of space.

"Captain, we are going to fall behind schedule by holding back those cargo transporters," complained Swedter.

"I don't want to take chances," Captain Brolocci explained, "those are not just my boys piloting those jump-jets. You never know how well some of those Warblers fly."

"How about using the bays in C Section? We can enter the workstation from the rear bays. That will leave you five forward sections to bring the jump-jets in." Francois paced in front of the hologram deck. He was getting impatient and losing his diplomatic air.

"And you don't see the problem." The captain was charming but firm in his statement. "It's not a matter of having enough space, we have thousands of miles of that, but some of these rocket jockeys don't realize there is a vast variance between the jet and rocket phase. One slip and they will miss the colony, go sailing away, and the last thing we need is for them to hit a damn luggage carrier," he pointed out. "I've been a pilot a long time, the difference could be as subtle as leaving your finger on the thruster a second too long. Or, realizing you did a second too late."

Francois Swedter was also a pilot. He had never flown anything the size of a jump-jet, as the captain had, but he knew more about those on board than Brolocci could imagine. He nodded to himself, to some coming up, their lives, or those of others, would not be as much a concern as the fate of their luggage. "Can't you extend the atmosphere around the colony, create a buffer zone, and then bring them in with the magnetic beams?"

"We are already doing that, the atmosphere has been increased a thousand feet at fifty P.S.I.," Brolocci said and pointed to the holograph. "The blue shading represents the air bubble as it stands. But see this thick circumference in red? That's our force field. We cannot increase the bubble anymore without making its magnetic containment too powerful to cross. As it is, we must selectively reduce its strength to provide the jump-jets a tunnel of low pressure. Look, most of them are already farther than halfway to the colony. Soon, you can resume normal operations."

Francois Swedter watched the representation of Colony 5 and all the little red planes creeping towards the giant ice-cream cone. The blue air engulfed the white globe in which he stood, round shapes were easier for creating the artificial gravity. Circular lasers powered its dynamos on several levels. The flight decks were gravity-free in the black and red cone that spiraled upward for miles. But soon, he would be gone from here and then he could put his knowledge of socio-politics to work for him. He would finally stop being a company name and start fulfilling his own destiny.

The New Eden Charter, created from chaotic legal proceedings involving everybody, produced a strange governing body; a free enterprising feudal republic. What the charter did stipulate was that first, all colonists received a parcel of land to do what they wished on, formed their own law in that territory, and conducted any business that suited them. Second, a planet-wide government comprising of colonists would decide the future price of the unsettled land and who bought it. Third, profits from the remaining sales would be split between U.S.I. and New Edeners, ninety/ten, of course. Fourth, all disputes were to be settled by majority rule. A system a lot like the one already regulating the colonies. The only difference was that U.S.I. could not claim the entire planet as theirs. Fortunes of unimaginable sums could be made by a smart person.

"I have to meet my successor in an hour." Captain Brolocci interrupted Swedter's dreams of grandeur momentarily.

"Control... Control, Prince Ashmir requesting flight doors of bay C-24 to be opened for takeoff," bade a heavy Arabic voice from the loudspeaker. He spoke the kind of English one learns instead of knows.

Francois reached over the console and took a hand mic, "Negative. We cannot clear any flights for takeoff at this time. Repeat... Negative... You have a holding pattern." *'Great, this is all I need,'* he thought, *'the prince wants to go joyriding.'*

"Control... Control... This is the Prince of Saudi Arabia and his ROYAL FAMILY, demanding clearance." His tone was sharp and forceful, gone were the carefully pronounced words.

Francois considered not replying, and for the moment, didn't. After all, the Saudis were not even sending anyone with Pegasus, as they refused to believe that life could exist anywhere else, no matter what kind of a planet they found.

A few moments later the call was repeated, and again denied.

'Why the hell did Ashmir and his royal family, all eighty-two of them, come here in the first place?' Francois wondered.

The entire gang had been in the colony for a week and had been nothing less than exasperating. Francois wished he could have refused them entrance then, but they were members of the Arabic Federation, and U.S.I. had a treaty with the Federation.

"Please be advised," he disclosed at last, "there is considerable danger in launching, due to heavy traffic in our space."

"I am a qualified pilot, who has flown in the Saudi Arabian Air Force during battle. I am not concerned with your dangers."

Charming guy, conceited too. These were not some little planes on the battlefield. Although, out there, it almost resembled one with the constantly moving air traffic. And it was all moving in one direction, so who did he think he was to demand otherwise and risk an incident? "That may be so, Prince Ashmir, but I am. Not only is your safety my responsibility, but so are the lives on those incoming ships. Now, sit tight until you are cleared." Francois Swedter was about to tell the technician at the console to cut the power in bay C-24 when a flash from the planet wiped the thought from his mind.

A morgue-like silence spread throughout the control room, as a black shroud crept across the face of the globe, everybody feeling in their hearts the burning realization of the nuclear blast. They stared at the huge monitor, some rising to their feet; others held fast onto their chairs, mouths agape, all in deep shock.

On the United States Space Defense Station, the scene was radically different. Warning lights glared, sirens blared, a flood of tactical information poured from speakers, and General Christopher Newton started barking out orders from the command deck.

"We have confirmation of twelve surface detonations. New York City, San Diego, Dallas… have all been incinerated by multi-megaton devices. Further reports confirm that major European and Soviet cities were also destroyed. There have been land launches, as well as submarine and battleship cruise missiles now in flight… Okay people, time to earn your pay. Remember, set your grid, and keep your bursts short and tight. Jesus, we have orders to commit! Total commitment, fire at will!"

Laser beams streaked from the station towards the surface, each ray stretching hundreds of feet in length and ten to twenty-feet across; compact waves of infrared radiation, three times as hot as the Sun's surface. Each missile they touched dissolved, every bomber and ship eradicated by the immense heat. Everything the invisible laser came into contact with evaporated in clouds of death, whitish blue trails left behind in the skies as testimony to the destructive power of the U. S. S. D. S.

Thousands of missiles were fired off and fired upon. Thousands were destroyed, but not all. Each time one reached its target, a telltale blinding flash was produced, followed by the white ring rising to the heavens.

"Open up the station," commanded Newton through his headset.

The building blocks of the station began spreading apart; it stretched out its arms, the laser cannons at the ends firing unceasingly.

"There are missiles heading for orbit," warned a radar operator.

"Section Seven, orbital projectiles are your babies. I want a tight low intensity beam. There are rocket ships out there and I don't want them roasted. What a day for U. S. I. to throw a party." General Newton stood on the command deck bathed in cool light, sweat running down from his sharp gray hairline in tiny rivulets.

Men encircled him, pounding at their control boards.

His eyes soaked in the horror show on the display screens around the room with a trained detachment. His voice as bland as the computer's, which poured out incessant information. "Lieutenant Charles, tighten up that beam. Find your grid, man, you are shooting at air! Remember, it may be your mother you are roasting with every misfire."

"Yes, Sir. Sorry, Sir."

"Don't apologize, mister, stick to the job at hand. Settle down and fire into the middle of your grid." Newton knew it was getting trickier to determine projectiles from projections, war crafts and weapons alike carried electronic devices designed to confuse both man and machine. Multiple images were produced and always shifting. "We should be getting a line of sight on Cosmo Red any moment. Section Four, mark up to full power. I want that station taken out swiftly."

Seconds later, the undetectable laser bolts raced through the darkness, erupting on the silvery skin of the enemy station. Pops and flashes continued to grow, both on Earth and in the space around her.

Newton knew the Kremlin had not pushed the button. He was positive the U.S. was not the inciter, either. Right now, he could not fathom who might be, he only knew for sure that he had strict orders to take them on if war broke out. And to that end, he surveyed the Russian station's disintegration.

Their stations were smaller and more mobile, but the Americans realized that mobility was useless in space or against laser weapons; they built theirs heavier to withstand bombardment. U.S.S.D.S. was even bigger with its cannons mounted on the arms away from the central station, which was protected by an energy field.

Lieutenant Charles studied the white dots that danced on his display. Punching computer keys, a lattice formed, and joining them. He set his range and dispersal controls, punched the fire button, and instantly, the dots vanished. Another missile vaporized.

Captain Brolocci charged back into the Control Center. "Command Twenty-four immediately," he shouted!

Nobody responded, all still immobile and transfixed in place.

The two hundred and forty-pound man shoved an operator half his size to the floor and started transmitting the commands. The room came alive at that instant.

"Wait! You can't launch Pegasus without someone on board." Francois tried desperately to reach him.

"We have no choice," retorted the Captain, "that station is not fortified. We have nothing to worry about from the rockets but those lasers will rip her apart. And don't you worry, we will evacuate the colony and rendezvous with her soon enough."

"Captain," a woman monitoring the Pegasus called out, "there are people on board. A Zackary Tops, an indentured, and Zuri Zauditu Mujaji, a technical advisor."

"Try to contact them, let them know they are moving out now."

"You are not going to turn Pegasus over to an indent…" protested Swedter.

"Would you rather see it burn up out there? Besides, I don't give a damn about their status. My duty is to protect that ship." Captain Brolocci keyed in the last of the emergency orders then switched to the intercom. "Attention all hands! Attention! Report to your assigned ships and prepare for immediate evacuation." He turned the radio to another frequency. "U.S. Space Defense Station...

Come in U. S. Space Defense Station, this is Captain Brolocci of the United Space Industries, Colony Five. Do you copy?"

"We copy, Captain. What is your condition?" asked the radio operator.

"Please be advised, we are preparing to evacuate. Repeating. United Space Industries Colony Five is preparing to evacuate and join Pegasus in-flight."

"Negative, Captain Brolocci. This is General Newton, please be advised that the situation is extremely hazardous. We are tracking multiple orbital projectiles, it would be safer for your people to stay put. We have routed your traffic to this base and are preparing to launch a squadron of rocket fighters to secure the area. Be advised that it will be better for you to increase your field's strength and maneuver into our umbrella."

The umbrella was the area behind the station that could be protected and the general certainly did not need or want more ships out there cluttering up an already crowded picture. The station was the closest to Earth at a mere ten thousand miles out. He had no fear they would come between him and the Earth, but there were small armed satellites, which they could potentially get tangled up with. Likewise, if one warhead exploded in the vicinity of a rocket ship, it would surely be destroyed. Only heavy armored plating and powerful field generators would save them, like those of the Colony itself.

The four Arabian Princes checked their watches with a mixture of urgency and nerves. They could wait no longer. Prince Ashmir hit the emergency launch button and four clouds of smoke formed in the doorway of bay C-24 as the door jettisoned into space. Their rocket's engines roared to life and the craft streaked away from the Colony before anyone knew what had ensued. Tails of flames wagged as the four princes and seventy-eight wives, children, and servants of their crew began chasing Pegasus. Several explosions rocked the Colony, cutting off power and adding to the already rampant madness. Large chunks of metal were flung into space, tiny human bodies followed them into the blackness.

"Mayday... Mayday... We have been hit..."

"Status report on Colony Five, sensor department," demanded the General as a close-up of the Colony appeared on the front screen. Smoke poured from several huge holes in the ball section, and part of the cone, near its top, had been blown off.

"Power is down; internal explosions were detected. Damage estimated at extreme, life supports are out, launch facilities impaired, back-up batteries at a mere ten percent. One spaceship got off just before the explosions."

"Before the explosions? Huh, identify craft and its heading, immediately" barked General Newton.

"Saudi Arabian Royal Flagship. With long range capability, Sir," a woman from the sensor department reported. "It's on an intercept course with Pegasus."

"Saudi, eh? Well, they won't catch her," he mused then said. "Arabian Flagship, this is General Christopher Newton of the United States Space Defense Station ordering you to cut your engines and submit to magnetic towing. You have sixty seconds to comply, or be destroyed. This is your only warning." The general had his position on display and any possible variation.

As soon as the transmission ended, Prince Ashmir kicked in everything his ship had then released a barrage of rocket fire at the station.

Seconds evaporated.

They burst into a fireball moments later, just as the prince was trying to block out the station's sensors. An old ploy which had no chance of success.

The flagship shimmered as its power field tried to deflect the X-rays, sparkles skipping across its surface while her circuits melted. The X-ray laser was nicknamed, 'The Frying Pan,' as in "out of the frying pan and into the fire." But unlike infrared lasers, this one cooked you from the inside out. Ninety seconds later, she was drifting, engines out, windows and external lights black, her crew dead.

"There is a squad dispatched. Should they recover the Arabian Ship, General, Sir?"

"Hell no," he thundered, "They are yesterday's news!" At least now, Newton had an idea of who may have fired the first shot. He had been receiving daily briefings to monitor Pegasus and its workstation for sabotage, but this was insane. Never would he have imagined this level of madness. But presently, there were more pressing concerns, like dealing with nuclear armed orbiting platforms.

Armament treaties of the last century forbade their existence, but they were out there nonetheless. Usually fifteen-feet long, they carried around a hundred small nuclear warheads, and had a total discharge period of three seconds. Naturally, they could fire in any direction, causing real undesirable trouble.

"Begin a full sweep pattern. Pull in those Colonies that are still outside the umbrella and close the net. I want engineering and medical teams dispatched to U.S.I. Five right away. Everybody stay sharp, this isn't over yet."

"What about Pegasus?" enquired the same sensor operator.

"Pegasus is on her own," the General commented gloomily.

He watched her image shrink steadily as she gained velocity. But his time for a sentimental goodbye was indeed short. More incoming warheads made their unsolicited presence felt with tremendous shockwaves buffeting the station. Total commitment meant they would be active until all unidentified or hostile elements had been vanquished. Judging from the intensity of the first strike, it was anyone's guess how long that would take.

CHAPTER FIVE

The potpourri of nuclear exchanges took both by surprise. The tranquility of the Observation Deck as shattered as that of Earth's.

"Zack! What was that? Did you see it? What is happening?"

Before I could answer her, the floodgates in my head burst open. Colombian memories rushed in, along with the smell of ionized air; the sight of blackened earth; the great pop as the air is sucked up; and the feeling of ants crawling all over me as a sea of flames burned through my mind.

"War... A war has started," I said, my voice sounding unlike my own, "It looks like someone has launched a major attack against the United States."

"But... I didn't see any rockets," Zuri quivered, "we should have seen them from here. You didn't see any, did you?"

I hadn't before the flashes, but there were some now, far too many from all around the globe. Something big had started. Really Big. "Maybe the warheads were dropped from one of the jump-jets, or they were suitcase bombs." I squeezed her hard, unable to take my eyes off the scene.

I could also see Zuri's reflection in the window, sheer panic superimposed on a ghastly backdrop. Black dots popped up on the face of Earth, and spread rapidly.

White strings snaked down to her; obviously, laser fire. The war was definitely on.

"They had to be suitcase-bombs," I continued. "Or else the U.S.'s early defenses would have picked them off. It looks pretty bad though, the conflict is spreading way too quickly. It's like everyone is fighting everybody."

Now, I understand the reason behind the big push, why the Company started double shifting. Someone must have known things were on shaky ground. They must have received threats, very serious ones. The Company had a far better Foreign-Affairs Bureau than any single country, due to the number of its offices worldwide. I'm sure Pegasus had stirred a big pot of beans. Today, that pot was boiling over.

There had been any number of nations opposed— for one reason or another—to the Pegasus Project from the very start. And the carving up of Earth as well as wholesale selling of a foreign uninhabited but pristine planet had turned some countries into bitter enemies. There were civil challenges as well, human rights groups launched a continuous campaign to disrupt and halt the building of the ship. But it was no longer court cases, injunctions, and military threats. It was war.

The smoke looked more like puffy clouds rather than rings, which meant laser beams were doing most of the damage. Even though the stations had been built for defense, they were definitely offensive structures now. Huge black clouds scarred the face of Earth, hiding cities, mountains and seas. Just a glimmer of red could be seen beneath them, which expanded into swirling shifting masses. First, the black ran through the bright blue, creating macabre shapes. Then it all changed to a sickly reddish black. Miles of Earth were blotted out. Huge chunks of land and sea hidden beneath the smoldering blanket of destruction.

Pegasus bolted and snapped me back to her world. The brightness from her engines firing wiped the glass clean. Sparks flew past us.

Zuri screamed, "My God, we've been hit!"

"No. I don't think so." I stared out, my mind racing. "We have been launched. Look out the other side, we are pulling out of the station. They are probably moving us to a safe distance." I wondered what a safe distance was, after all, a laser beam can travel hundreds of thousands of miles in a matter of seconds. But after what felt like a mere moment, we were surrounded by the blackness.

The Moon raced towards us and Earth was fading in its death shroud.

I drifted around the deck, drawn to the best possible view of the conflict and watched a rocket-ship take off from Colony 5, just before it belched fire and smoke. Minutes later, the ship started flipping like a fish thrown upon the shore to catch its last breath. The bright lights of rocket-ships and missiles striped the ever-growing black cloud. A fiery sea grew under that blanket.

I found myself sweating. In Colombia, I felt the heat even behind the battle-shields. When we did one, a SNIP, the walls turned white from the back-flash. We would sweat as if we had just stepped into a sauna, like I was doing now. I know the waves can't reach us, not yet, and Pegasus has skin stronger than a battle-shield, but a clammy wetness ran down my back anyway. The flashes continued and the little sunspots they left stung like hell. They distorted my vision with tears I did not want to shed.

The black cloud engulfed the planet and streamed spaceward, growing wildly just as life itself does, tentacles leaping from its swirling body. It was a hungry beast consuming the world, space stations, colonies, and atomic explosions, laser fire and all.

Six hours. Just six short hours and the Twenty-First Century expired, vanishing into the gloom of space. Humanity's resting place was marked by a black noxious cloud with a faint warm glow deep within. It was April 22, 2057, Earth Day.

I don't know how long I stood on the Observation Deck. The pain that started out as a burning sensation in my feet now reached up my legs. I felt it the worst in the back of my knees. I sat back in a deep soft chair, I shot up, relieved of the pain for a moment, then settled down again. I closed my eyes but the sunspots attacked with savage fury. I had to fight back those horrible thoughts, trying to escape my frenzied sub-consciousness.

Zuri had fled some time ago, but where did she go? She must be devastated by this time. The shock had twisted her pretty smile into a wide-eyed gape. Several times I gave her a little shake or tight squeeze to keep her breathing. I don't know if she realizes that everyone on Earth, by now, is dead, and I don't want to mention it either. I don't know if she is still watching. The Earth has become too small, dark, and insignificant at this distance.

'I'd better find her, no telling what's on her mind.' "Zuri, can you hear me? It's Zack," I spoke softly into the ship's communicator, artificially so, "are you OK?"

"Yeah, I'm alright."

I could hear sobs.

"I'm on the Control Deck," her voice was lifeless, "on the Bridge."

"Well, don't touch anything..."

"Doesn't matter, the controls are locked in," she sighed.

"I'm on my way. And don't worry..." I thought for a few seconds, my finger steadfast on the mic key. There should have been more to say, but nothing came out.

I solemnly headed for a transport car, my thoughts coming to mind very dimly. Everything looked strange, as if I had just got off a plane in a foreign country. I began to wonder if I was okay. I closed my eyes to clear my pounding head and the sunspots came rushing back.

When I stepped out of the car, Zuri was sitting at the communication station, her fists pounding on the channels keyboard repeatedly. She shouted over and over at the glossy machinery, its square LED's keys lighting up frantically, "Hello... This is Pegasus... Somebody, please acknowledge!"

So intent was she in her mission to reach someone, anyone, big or small, that she didn't notice I was standing behind her. Her tear-streaked reflection confirmed what I feared. I placed my hands firmly on her arms to stop their aimless flailing. Her hands clenched tightly at some invisible lifeline, and so strong was her grip that her fingertips were fire red. I could feel her trembling as I tried to lift her from the chair, where she was solidly planted before the communication console, her body stiff, as if rigor mortis had set in. She was locked in this sitting position and vibrating so wildly, her body almost hummed.

Had to snap her out of the state of shock. "Zuri... Zuri." I shouted.

She mumbled and kept trying to transmit.

"Zuri, no one is going to answer, even if they can hear you. Nobody will risk revealing their position. Besides, the radiation will make communications impossible on any frequency, other than laser transmission."

She started to calm down. And then it all came pouring out, endless tears, trembling lips, and the shaky voice. "How could they? And who started it? Oh God, Zack, what are we going to do?"

Each question was a bullet. She needed me now, and I was supposed to be strong for her sake, but I was scared senseless too, and likewise, did not have clear answers. "Don't worry, we have been set on automatic. The crew must have a plan for catching up with us when it becomes safe."

For the first time, I lied to her. I had seen Colony 5 rocked by explosions, I hoped she had not. That was why they had not answered; the damage must have been extensive.

I managed to put up a strong front. "We are going to be all right. This ship can accommodate a hundred thousand people." That I was sure of.

"But we are the only ones left." The thought was obviously terrifying.

"We are not the only people left," I tried hard to smile. I held her in my arms, she moaned, and it made me warm. "Someone must have survived the Exchange. I know for a fact the U.S. has several huge underground facilities. And there are the colonies, the settlement on Mars, and those at the Belt."

"Yes, I realize that," she wiped her burning eyes. "But we are on our way to Alpha Centauri. The escape rockets of Colony 5 will have to push hard just to reach Mars. If they can't catch up to us, we will be quite alone when we arrive at New Eden. We've got to stop, or get off."

"I don't know how to stop this ship. And if we left, where would we go? There is nowhere safer than right here, right now. It will be kind of like Adam and Eve when we reach New Eden." This time I did smile a big toothy one for her. "I kinda like that idea."

She squeezed me, so hard I felt dizzy.

We cleared the communication boards and opened all frequencies, including the laser channels. We tied in the ship's intercom; in case anyone does contact us, we can answer from anywhere in Pegasus. I kept assuring her the escape rockets of Colony 5 would do so soon. But every time I said it, a picture of flames shooting from the colony materialized. I had seen one ship get off, but it seemed to have floundered, or lose control. They might not have been real pilots.

I suggested, and Zuri hastily agreed, to go back to the brook where we had our picnic. There, we could collect ourselves. Think. Come up with a plan of action. Also, I felt the calm surroundings would help Zuri with this catastrophe. I hoped it would help me too. I felt that at any moment, the floor was going to drop out, and I would find myself alone, drifting away. But worst of all, powerless.

The babbling brook did all the talking. We lay back, watching the artificial sun crossing the artificial sky. We watched the imitation clouds drifting by on the imitation breeze. I could not enjoy them as I did before and I wondered if I could ever again find the solace this place had held. I refused to close my eyes. I knew they were waiting for me, those damn sunspots. I guess I fought them off until exhaustion won.

I woke alone. Zack must have gone back to the bridge. I wondered how long I had been asleep, or for that matter, when I went to sleep. I realized time will now be of extreme importance because every second takes us deeper into space. It was 5 p.m.; I slept almost an entire day. "Zack, can you hear me?"

"Yes, I'm on the bridge."

"OK. I'll be right there."

Suddenly, I felt dirty. Not the normal morning breath, but the type of feeling one gets from lice, so tiny they're invisible, crawling all over me. A shower was what I desperately needed and I headed for our unit. The hot water beat hard on my face, almost burning it; I guess it was controlled too. They designed Pegasus to be accident proof.

The hot water washed away the bugs, but only for the moment; before I could dry off they were back creeping up and down my arms, legs, and body. Back into the shower I went, trying in vain to kill them. After a while, a long while, I joined Zack on the bridge. The bugs were still there, but I tried hard not to think of them.

"What have you found out?" Zuri asked, expecting to hear the crew was on their way.

"The radio is still dead," I told her flatly. "We can't gain control of Pegasus until she reaches her emergency destination. I've been reading these emergency procedures for hours."

"Then… how are they going to catch us?"

"I don't know." I avoided her ghastly eyes. "But they must have had some kind of plan in mind when they launched us. We will just have to sit and wait until they contact us. I'm sure we will hear from them in a day or two."

"Why can't we get a message to them?"

"We need a security clearance to operate the bridge controls. But all is not lost; we may have a chance to gain control of the ship after the security time-check has been reached."

"When will that be?"

I could feel the anxiety swelling inside her, knowing she is deathly afraid of solitude.

Most of her life, it was just Zuri and her father and he had been busy more often than she cared to remember. When he died, so did a big chunk of her. Not as if a part of her had been taken away, it was more a dire sense that long waited to come to pass. It was a bad time for her.

'Very bad, indeed,' she thought, *'No, I can't think of that. I won't, not this time. Besides, I have Zack, and he is everything.'*

"Zuri, are you listening?"

Her mind was far away.

I repeated myself when I gained her attention. "You have to learn all there is to know about the communications system and I am going to concentrate on the security and navigation systems. After all, once we take Pegasus off automatic we will have to plot a course back to Earth. I know the Company; some of them should have survived."

"How are we going to learn something that takes five years to fully comprehend in a few days? We will be orbiting New Eden before we can learn to control her!"

"I've done some thinking in these few hours. Logically speaking, our destination cannot be New Eden. First, why have an emergency code for someplace we are already going to? Second, why send the ship out if your chances of a rendezvous are so small. They probably got us on a pattern that will move us to a safe distance from Earth and hold. Or swing us around in a huge circle, so we can pick them up after the situation settles down."

"Makes sense to me," she smiled, this time like she did before the Exchange. She was adjusting. Zuri had an indomitable spirit, all it took was a little spark of hope.

I was glad to give it to her. "From what I understand, so far, one of us must be on the bridge at all times. When a time-check is called for, we can access the main computer. That is the only way to gain control of the ship. If we miss a time-check, we will have to wait until the next one to interface with the security system, and we can only do that through the bridge computer."

"Maybe we can get my little friend to help us out." She was talking about her communications robot. "He can monitor the bridge computer and alert us when it's time. How much time do we need to reach the bridge?"

"I don't know yet."

I could see where she was coming from. But this also showed she was feeling better, more in control of herself. That is also the decision I made earlier, to keep in control. It had hit me like lightning by the river; we have enough supplies to last several lifetimes. Hence, the best plan of action is to learn all we can about this ship. By learning how it operates, we will be able to govern our lives and future.

But it doesn't really matter whether there is anybody left on Earth or not, once we operate Pegasus, we can go anywhere, or nowhere. We can tell all those people at the far posts to join us. But first, we have a lot of learning to do and the best place for the job is the Teacher.

"I think we should study in shifts," I suggested. "One person in the Teacher while the other watches the bridge. You see, I don't know how long the intervals between time-checks are; it could be hours, days, or months even."

"But if we don't know what to do when the time-check does come up, then what is the sense of being there?" Zuri reasoned.

She had a point, perhaps we should cram together. Then when we computed the time schedule, we would have a clear-cut plan.

I timed the trip as we headed for the Teacher. The room of audio-video equipment that was collectively known as the Teacher, was in the body section. It was nearly the last deck of the ship and four minutes from the bridge.

The Teacher presented its own problems; volumes of instructions had to be read just to start up the system. Unfortunately, the technicians had not been due to bring the system online for another week. But once it was running, the Teacher could instruct us on any of Pegasus' systems as well as any other subject.

"Just for the record," I said as we poured through the manuals, "there are six thousand individual systems on board."

"Uh huh."

It didn't really mean much to either of us, I just said it to pass the time.

CHAPTER SIX

I didn't bother keeping track of time and now I don't recall precisely if it has been a week or a month since the Exchange. We buried ourselves in reading and studying the systems, and once we figured out how to boot the Teacher, she taught us the rest, including how to access the various learning modes. We ate, drank, and slept in the Teacher.

We utilized the sleep mode as well as transcendental hypnotic learning, especially when it came to things that went far beyond our comprehension. Zuri's little bot came in extremely handy, not only as our extra ears, but hands and feet also. It allowed me to totally exist with the Teacher, and still I couldn't learn fast enough. The security system had thousands of bridges, different criteria for every occasion. I had to rely on the Teacher to find the quickest way to present it.

Zuri and I have hardly spoken for a while, even though we spend entire days together. Our eyes meet sometimes, like strangers, unable to find that first word. We talk either to the Teacher or the bot, never each other. And in those instants when we do pass each other, we are so careful not to touch. Afraid, I guess, that we might exploded. Like the explosions that still reverberate nightly through my dreams. Those damn sunspots swarm my brain when Teacher turns her back. I have to find a way to beat them. Rid myself of those fireflies that buzz my quiet moments.

I began slipping away from the Teacher; first, to check some of the other systems and bring them online. I had to bring up the habitats' controls and monitors, so the different environments could flourish. They had been in a static phase when the Exchange took place. These environments are fully segregated by electronic signals to protect the populations, and the signals can reap havoc on the nervous systems of the different animals, as they create an invisible barrier. The blocks can be shut down from time to time to control the population of the habitats. Every aspect of life on Pegasus is monitored and controlled. I began to realize that I too was being monitored and controlled. Monitored by the bot and controlled by the Teacher.

I sought refuge in the green habitats. An afternoon swim in the lake on Deck 17 is deeply relaxing. Finches race from tree to tree singing. Here, things are real. Life is real. Fish, birds, trees, and above all, noise. Because that's what life is, sounds. The softest crackle of a leaf landing on the ground, the gentle scurrying of a bunny… that is reality.

The squirrel's peek-a-boo life is just right. He does not care if his tree is planted on Deck 17. The trout in the lake cannot fathom that his water travels five hundred miles a day to be vaporized and condensed again. The orange-breasted finch isn't disturbed by the high-pitched hawk's cry that turns him from the webbed ceiling of the habitat. But I am. Somewhere inside, it bothers me. And after a while, I find this quiet little pain deep in the back of my neck pushing me from this respite.

When I leave, it's back to the Teacher I go. All the time monitored and controlled. Once in a while, I'll stop by the bridge. Usually, if she is not with the Teacher, Zuri goes there. I'll find her at one of the consoles working hard. I never disturb her, just observe from the Captain's Walk overhead. Or I'll stand behind her on the bridge floor, quietly, out of sight. All the huge monitors have the same message, "Emergency Procedure: Auto Control Engaged."

Zuri managed to pull up our status on one of the console's screens. The numbers and words are unintelligible from this distance. She worked for hours at the keyboard without much results, then, took out her laser pen and zapped the telecommunication relays. The act seemed perfectly all right to me at first, but when all the monitors went black, she ran to the Teacher. I reached the Teacher a few minutes after her, delayed by the awesome sight of the bridge's total blackout. She was talking to the Teacher, asking for the layout to the system. That's when it hit me as an odd thing to do.

A few days later she was back on the bridge, which was operating again thanks to the spiders. She seemed quite content. Possibly, she needed to blow off some anger, blast the machine one good time to let them know she was still in charge. She can't hurt them. Maybe she wants to but the spiders come and undo the damage she has done. They don't need to be called, no egg to mark the spot, they just come. Monitored and controlled.

Or perhaps, she is trying to escape that feeling like I do in the habitats. I have taken to racing through the habitats, nude. I don't really know why, I just do. It feels good to run. I go from scene to scene, forest to desert, mountains to beaches, and jungle to tundra. All the different eyes stalking me and waiting to take control.

But I finally know what I must do, I must take control from the Teacher. I am very much aware she will not relinquish her power easily, so I have a hell of fight on my hands. I have come to know the Teacher, and I know she is rooted deep inside my head.

Just about the time I reached Deck 22, it struck. Pressure built in my ears from something swelling within my brain. It broke my stride and threw me to the ground. I grasped and tore at the tall swaying grass, desperately trying to crawl away from the pain. It dug deeper as I thrashed about. I caught a glimpse of something in the prairie, between the plunges of bloody knives into my head. Somehow, and with great difficulty, I managed to pull myself from Deck 22.

It took a long time to walk back to the Teacher. I plopped down, sighing low and slow. "Layout and requirements of Deck Twenty-two."

The Teacher responded warmly, in a voice nearly like my mother's. "Deck Twenty-two has dangerous life forms. No entry without an Alpha-transmitter is permitted."

I should get back to the lake, clean up, and perhaps catch a fish or rabbit for dinner. Fresh catch is so much better than what the bot brings Zuri. I refuse to eat that processed crap anymore.

When I got back to the Teacher, Zuri was all smiles. It seemed so unreal, her face radiated a new glow I have never seen, her manner childlike.

She grabbed my arm as I entered and dragged me to the video terminal on the far side of the room.

"I broke the security blackout," she practically shouted in my ear.

"That is great," I was stunned, "we can finally take control..."

"Huh... wait a second," Zuri sounded embarrassed, "we don't have control. What I meant was that I accessed some information about the emergency procedures we are under. Here, see for yourself."

I read the screen, noticing the way she looked at me, surprised to say the least. I realized this was the first time she really saw me in weeks.

"So by blowing up the relays, you have discovered we are heading for Mars."

"Yes. Once they were gone, the Teacher had to tell me what they were monitoring. We have been tracking the Martian Colony's location beacon since we left."

That makes sense, as the Mars Colony is well within reach of any ship U.S.I. had at Colony 5. They can meet us there in a couple of months with no problems. Except for the one large explosion I cannot forget seeing the day of the Exchange. I am sure they did not reckon that in when they launched us on our way to Mars.

She had a worried look in her eyes. I could tell she was apprehensive about being with me. The blood from my rabbit dinner had dried in my beard.

"We have been traveling for nine and a half weeks." She was trying hard to speak naturally now. "Zack, we should be halfway there. I tried to contact the colony, but that damn emergency procedure won't allow any outgoing transmissions. At least not on any of the bands I've tried so far."

His eyes flitted back and forth while I spoke and I wondered if I was making any sense at all. I couldn't help feeling sorry for him; he had lost a lot more than I did that day. I had no family to torture my mind. Zack was not so lucky. I saw him slipping away those first few days, and how I wish I could have helped. He never said anything about them, but their deaths must be tearing his heart apart. He mumbled something and I asked him to repeat it.

"I think I know how to gain control of the ship without waiting until we get to Mars."

"That's great!" I said.

He brushed some red flakes from his face.

I assumed it was blood, although, I couldn't imagine where it came from.

Zack turned slightly to the left, probably ashamed to face me in that state.

I asked him about his plan, trying to mask the fear I had of him, and for him.

"I'll show you when it's worked out."

That night I couldn't shake the dread building inside of me. It wasn't the nudity that shocked me; it was the wildness in his eyes. And I could not help wondering, where the hell have I been? We have seen each other daily, hours at a time, but I had not noticed until now. Why? Had I been so absorbed by Pegasus that I forgot to pay attention to everything else around me? Whereas Zack had stripped himself of all reminders of civilization, I buried myself in a grave of computers.

Sometimes, I spent as much as seventy-two hours wired to the Teacher, its electrodes taped to my forehead. The optic cups blocking out real existence and transmitting its garbage to color my vision. I felt my left ear; yes, it was still there, the radio receiver that was living off me like a parasite. Angrily, I threw it to the floor. Its tiny metallic body bounced softly on the carpet, unharmed. I ran from the Teacher. Ran until I caught sight of myself in the black glass doors of a living unit.

I was thin, but not gaunt, like a zombie, black circles ringing my eyes from lack of sleep. My shoulders, elbows, and knees protruded from my waning limbs. My own ghostly appearance replaced my image of Zack, which I had feared so much. Hell, at least Zack looked healthy, crazy, yes, but strong.

I thought, *a few more days like this, and I'll be dead of malnutrition.*

It was two days before I heard from him again. He called me over the intercom to meet him for some "real food". He must have noticed my condition too.

I felt strange about this meeting, a few thoughts kept popping into my mind. First, Zack hasn't used the ship's intercom in over a month. His voice sounded unreal, mechanical, as we had barely grunted to or at each other in weeks. Second, there was that damn dream last night.

I was fighting my way through some tall grass, like when I was six in Kivu. I could hear the drums beating out a furious and angry cadence. They got so loud that each thump nearly knocked me off my feet. I was scared, but of what, I didn't know. Finally, I broke out into a clearing. Zack was there, dressed in skins, bones, and feathers, like an ancestral warrior, and he did not see me as I ran to him. His head down, he repeatedly speared some kind of animal at his feet. At last, I was within reach of his blood-splattered body when a low moan rose between us. Slowly looking down, I saw the mutilated body of an animal with the anguished head of my father! Zack, smiling weirdly, his eyes wild as before, lunged for me. I woke terrified.

Before meeting Zack on Deck 18, I stopped at the security office, grabbed a small laser pistol from the arms cabinet, and tucked it away under my robes.

Zack was waiting near a roaring campfire. A skinned lamb suspended above the fire sent a beautiful aroma through the air. The smoke danced among the birch trees and fanned out high overhead. Zack was dressed in the company's jumpsuit, and although the legs were cut off at the knees, and the sleeves torn from his shoulders, he looked normal.

Zuri arrived at the gateway between decks. Each gateway is lined from end to end on the ground and ceiling with rows of red and green lights. Some gateways have walls a few yards on either end, but most, like this one, are open. Only an electronic barrier to mark the end of one habitat and the start of the next.

"Hi," Zuri greeted, still nervous, but not as afraid. "A barbecue picnic is a nice idea."

"Yeah, you look like you can use a good meal." I laughed a little but then thought it didn't sound quite right. "Sorry, I didn't mean that. Anyway, we have fresh picked fruits here, some salad I made with salmon, and delicious roasted lamb. I have become somewhat of a good cook these days." I lied, I've been eating most of my meals raw.

"So I see. Is this a celebration, or something?"

"Kinda," I could sense she was apprehensive. "It's a getting-to-know-you-again dinner. I figure when we get to Mars there will be about five thousand people to pick up, so we won't have this time to be alone again. And after all that has transpired, I am worried about you. And I know you have some doubts about me... Hell, I have doubts about me."

She chuckled and felt her side. Then her gaze dropped to the ground.

I paused and we sat down side by side. The fire was hissing and crackling loudly, she watched it intently, no doubt to avoid looking at me.

I said softly, "You know I will never harm you, Zuri. You are all I want in this life. And you don't need that gun, not for me anyway, but if it makes you feel safe then keep it."

I could tell she was ashamed.

I felt terrible; this was not what I had planned.

"This is... this is not because of you," she stuttered, "I am afraid of the animals in these habitats."

"Oh," I wanted to believe her. "But no need to worry about any of the life forms on these decks. The dangerous ones start at deck twenty-two, a couple of levels below us."

"How did you know I had a laser?" Zuri was finishing off another banana.

I was sloppily eating a cantaloupe and de-juiced my mouth with the back of my hand.

She winced at the crude move and tore a corner from her robe. "Here," she said and wiped my face.

Electricity dazzled my mind. This was the first time we touched in so long and I could see the effect on her too. It was great.

"Uh, I'm the Acting Security Officer," I responded to her question. "Pegasus alerted me when you went to the armory."

"Oh, I didn't know that."

"I'm also the Acting Captain." I officially informed her. "You're the Acting First Officer and Navigator." I wondered if I should tell her my plan but things were starting to flow between us. I quickly decided against it and passed her a huge hunk of lamb.

"I hope we don't have to eat all this food now."

We laughed. This was the best time we had together in months and we talked for hours. I explained how the Emergency Procedures allowed me to name us as temporary officers, but how those very same rules barred us from altering Pegasus' basic functions.

"That is why," I continued, "you can get a fix on our heading, but can't send them a message to tell them we're coming. We are under silent navigation and I have a feeling our arrival on Mars will be a complete surprise to the colonists. I don't even know if the ship will stop there. For all we know, it will swing around and head straight back to Earth."

"What do you think the colonists will be doing? Do you think they know?"

I hadn't thought about it yet. "Not sure what they already know but they might. If not, when they see us it will be obvious what occurred. And we both know they are not self-sufficient. Their supplies will only hold out two years, maybe three… max."

"They might panic," she summarized, "or head back to Earth."

"If they left for Earth the very next day, we won't pass them for another month. Maybe." They had Class IV rocket drivers, not exactly the fastest things in space travels.

The conversation brought out the warmth of skin touching skin. The sensations of human contact. Feelings long dead, also felt a rebirth of hope. The malignancy of the old world had finally been dispelled. Soft moans sang to the music of the campfire. Pungent odors of burning meat were fueled by passion. And the wonderful glow reflected by moist skin, illuminated the forest clearing. Glistening eyes and feverish tongues, all this and more consumed us. Existence had died and living had returned. The song of night played.

I worked like a madman for the next few days, had to beat the security system before we reach Mars. Zuri seems to take comfort in knowing where we are going, the thought of being on a runaway horse had terrified her. But for me, knowing where we are headed changes nothing. I want full control of the ship and I am sure the only way to take command is by creating a situation that Pegasus cannot handle.

I spent a lot of time working on the alpha transmitters, and a lot of time running. Running made me feel great, cleared my head, and kept those nasty little buggers out. With my alpha box on, I could race the lions, tigers, and other big cats of Deck 22. They would initiate the pursuit, but as they closed in for the kill, the alpha box drove the cats crazy, chasing them away.

I was working on a box that would allow them not only to stalk and close in, but also make the kill. Naturally,

I have to time the attack, so I know when Pegasus will take over to prevent it. After much thought and scheming, I was ready for a test.

The knee-high grass waved and parted, telltale signs that a cat was nearby. About one hundred yards from the exit I threw my alpha box away. The pain that accompanied the shield-less in this habitat was an old friend to me now. The bubble in the grass raced towards me.

"Security Officer, human in danger on Deck Twenty-two." The tiny earphone told me nothing I didn't already grasp.

I took off for the portal, as Deck Twenty-two is a walled habitat. All the exercise has me in great shape, but I am not fast enough to beat a lion. Its roar had my heart pounding. I was about twenty-five yards from the barrier zone. *'Oh, no!'* I thought, *'I am going to make it.'* I looked back to see the cat's tan mane rising out of the thick grass barely ten-feet away.

At the sight of its huge head and bared dagger-like teeth, I froze. Fear stiffened every muscle in me, as the cat sailed hungrily towards its dinner. But instead of the lion ripping me to shreds, he fell lifeless before me. Cautiously I touched his side, finding its breathing and heartbeat nearly stopped.

"Security Officer, the danger has passed."

Pegasus had paralyzed the animal and saved my life. I quickly made it out the portal. The pain was gone and I watched the bubble slowly work its way deeper into the savanna's foliage.

Zack called me to Deck 19 to go for a swim. Things had been rather different for the past two weeks. I managed to access the long-range spectrometer and spent most of the day looking for ships. It was a boring task, but it did give me something to do, so I was very happy when Zack suggested the beach. It has been two years since we had gone near the ocean back on Earth.

The sands stretched a quarter mile from the portal to the waterline. Palm trees ran a half mile on both sides of the doorway. The crystal blue water spread out to a depth of two hundred feet at the one mile marker, and remained at that depth for another mile. Deck 19 was Pegasus' primary aquarium, home to two thousand species of marine life forms.

Zack was late and he had not said where on the beach to meet him. I walked along the shoreline, letting the waves just submerge my sandals. The water rolled to the rhythm of Pegasus like a heartbeat, the whitecaps effervescing their beauty to the warm air. It was perfect, like all the other worlds on this ship. Never too cold or too hot, the wind never too strong, always just perfect. That was Pegasus' one flaw.

In an instant, my thoughts were drawn to a time long ago. I was whisked away to my nomadic childhood by a familiar sound, the gut-wrenching growl of a lion. Instincts born in the bush country dropped me to all fours. My eyes narrowed, tracking the tree line for movement.

I realized the water would not save me; a hungry lion will swim for his dinner. I had to make it across the open beach back to the exit. A cold tingle at my side reminded me of the laser pistol I still carried.

The other night raised a new fear, pirates. Since most of the outposts are not self-sustaining, they depend on supply ships. Ships sent from Earth. The ships that will not be coming anymore. Now, I was real glad I've been carrying it, for fear against being boarded.

I had to move slow and low, looking out for the lion. The growl grew louder but I couldn't locate the portal. It was somewhere amongst the palms and so was that lion.

"Zack! Where the hell are you?" I shouted. There was no answer.

Another roar brought up all the terrifying memories.

I screamed into the communicator around my neck, "Zack! Zack, I need you! Help!"

Still there was no response. Then the dream came back, but this time, it was Zack's face and his bloody body I envisioned. The lion came leaping across the sand, covering a lot of ground quickly. I ran for the trees. Arms and legs pumping furiously, afraid to look back, I headed into the palms. The crunching of the dry leaves warned me not to stop.

The thunder of its voice told me it was close, and ready to kill. I spun around, pulled, and pressed the fire button on the laser pistol. Red letters flashed on its fat black top, "Unmatched Print."

The lion charged.

"Security Officer, human life form in danger on Deck Nineteen." Pegasus' electronic voice rang in my ear. Through binoculars, I saw Zuri standing stunned. I was high in a palm, the lion only eighty yards from her and closing fast.

"Electronic paralyzation ineffective. Situation… Critical."

'*I am taking an enormous gamble,*' I watched the beast close in on Zuri.

The alpha transmitter I had strapped to the feline's neck nullified Pegasus' control. The numbers on the binoculars' lens dropped rapidly.

"Emergency Condition on Deck Nineteen. Security Officer, respond immediately!"

"Finally," I said with twenty-yards separating my love from death. "This is acting Security Officer Zackary

Tops, Pegasus stand down from all Emergency Procedures. Upgrade all acting ranks to full commission."

"Done."

My fingers squeezed the transmit button on a second alpha box I had modified. The lion leaped, extending its massive claws.

Hot flames ripped through my head, everything was lost.

CHAPTER SEVEN

I awoke back in our living unit with two men driving nails through my head, or so I thought. The pain was intolerable.

"How are you feeling?" asked Zack. He was sitting in a chair by the bed; seemed like he had been there a long time.

"OK, I think. Do you remember crash training?" I couldn't describe how I really felt, although, after those exercises I felt like I do now.

"Drink this." He handed me a cup of yellow liquid. "It will alleviate the effects of the neuro-paralyzer. Don't try to move or talk for a while."

"What happened?" My whole body ached as I sat up to drink.

"We are now in full control of Pegasus, First Mate Zuri Mujaji. I am sorry I had to use you like that, but I didn't want you to think that I had gone completely insane."

"You mean you released that lion!" I was shocked. "Why, Zack?"

"I had to create a situation Pegasus could not handle. I fixed one of the alpha transmitters to paralyze the lion on a human frequency. I knew Pegasus wouldn't use that frequency; therefore, it was powerless to stop the attack. When the emergency arose, it had to turn control over to me. I knocked the both of you out, well, the three of us, and when I awoke I brought you here. Then I removed the transmitter and sent the lion back to his domain."

"How did you know you would wake up before the lion did?"

"I had a second neurotransmitter on. One that would revive me within a minute of being knocked out. Sort of a defibrillator to the tenth power, and the excruciating pain was worth it. Now, we are in control. But there is a second reason why I kept my plan from you. If you knew I was going to save you, you might not have given me enough time to take control."

"What did you do to my zapper, Zack? The laser didn't work," I croaked in agony.

"Oh, yeah," he smiled, "those things were preset for the security team. The trigger reads the fingerprint patterns, yours are not in its memory. This is good, Zuri, if you had blasted that lion, we wouldn't have been able to gain control. And Zuri, you were never in any real danger, I could have knocked out the lion at any time. Anyway, here's your laser, I've set it up for you."

"Great, what good is the stupid thing now," I flared.

"Well, there still is the possibility of pirates, you know."

The pain subsided, the yellow liquid was working.

Zack told me we were still on course to Mars and he had now instructed Pegasus to orbit over the colony when we arrived. He also started transmitting a continuous message to them, but was disturbed because we had not yet received a reply. He felt something was amiss. We increased our speed, so we could reach the planet in a week.

It was a week of nightmares for me. Memories of children being carried off in those jaws of death plagued my sleep. The whole village haplessly following the trails of blood left by my playmates. Those were horrible times and they came back to me with a vile vividness. Zack could not imagine the terror he unleashed. No one knew, I never talked about those days in the bush. I had locked them away. Forever. I hoped.

I could feel the dry hot air on my face. It crackled, as did the dry grass under my feet. The women, in their colorful wraps, stood waist deep in the pale brown swaying sea, keeping constant watch for the cats as we played in the murky water. Beyond the grass fields were the white limestone houses of the village. Small banyan and large baobab trees dotted the plains. They were transplanted in the region for food and shade by Daddy.

They eased the drought in the south region with their expansive root systems, but they also gave refuge to the cats of prey. That is always the way of Nature, nothing is gained without sacrifice. So, the women stood watch under the blazing sun, and waited for another of their babies to be carried away. Sometimes, they managed to fire a shot from the spear-like stinger rods they held. But even when hit by the electric bolt, the lions would jump up and roll over in pain, then they would dash away with their young prey gripped firmly between their jaws.

No sooner did I awaken from one terrible dream then another started. Zack was in some, sitting in the sparse branches of a fatted baobab tree, looking as twisted as the tree, like a demented demon. His eyes were blazing, hair wild, his face and body wet and shiny blood red. In some of the dreams, that cat sat with him. Sometimes, the trees were full of felines. I called his name, pleading for him to rescue me. Then, all at once, they pounced, their claws tearing at my body. I woke up two or three times a night and Zack was always ready to comfort me.

During the day, we sat at the scanners looking for others. Interplanetary space is not overrun with people or ships. Outside of the earth orbiting stations, the mining facility on Mars is the largest colony, housing a mere five thousand.

Most people live on, or near Earth. Well... they used to. The other ships sailing this black sea average ten-member crews. The rockets came from different individuals having different needs, and most did not carry the long-range scanners that would permit them to find a ship in this eternal sea. Or the powerful micro beams to transmit over the millions of miles of darkness.

Pegasus is so equipped. If there is anyone out here, we will have to find them ourselves, but it is frustratingly difficult. We scan for energy fluctuations, or even, an alloy spectrum. An energy fluctuation can mean a rocket engine firing or shutting down. Ships use their engines only at take-off and course changes. At all other times, they glide through the timeless night appearing as pieces of cosmic debris.

The spectrum analysis told us the chemical components of those pieces. Also, it informed us of changes in the surrounding electric fields. It was pretty to watch, however, there was nothing to see.

We rejoiced at reaching the colony, though, I was still concerned that we had received no reply. The colonists should have picked up Pegasus a hundred hours ago. As a precaution, a good one under these circumstances, we established a high orbit. At ten thousand miles, they could not fire on us, and it gave us a reasonable head start if they did.

Zuri wanted to take a jump-jet down right away. I convinced her we should scan the facility first and wait for a response. After we learn all we can from the scanners then we can go down if necessary.

"What could be wrong?" she asked innocently.

"A lot of things," I told her on the observation deck.

The colony was laid out in a triangle. Small bubbles packed close together comprised one point. The other half of the pyramid had long rectangles fanning out to the south. The landing field was thirty miles from the north point. Three glass tubes ran from the launch pads to the main dome. Two class-four rockets stood in their place.

"It would not make sense for them to leave in cargo-haulers like those. Maybe, nothing is wrong... it could also simply be that the transmitter is broken... or turned off."

"But," Zuri insisted, "why can't we land in a jump-jet?"

"Suppose they are waiting to ambush us? I just don't want to rush into the unknown. What if they have been ambushed themselves?"

"That's ridiculous," she laughed at my suggestions. "Our crew, if we had the full contingent, would outnumber them six to one. And they have no knowledge of our situation."

"Hell, after the Exchange, they could be waiting to commandeer anything that comes along. We must protect Pegasus, it's our only means of survival. Believe me, others will view it as their only hope too!"

"It is," Zuri's gaze froze me to the bone, "this ship can provide for a hundred thousand people. I seriously doubt we can find those many now." The look said it all, she didn't care who we found, anybody would be alright.

I did not mind sharing Pegasus with those who were willing to share but there were major decisions to make, such as, where do we go from here? And who should decide? Me? Should we go on to New Eden? Or perhaps back to Earth, to search for survivors? I shook that responsibility right out of my head.

Sipping on a brandy, I realized I was getting way ahead of the problem. I know that I must descend to the colony but for now, I'll sip my drink, scrutinize their butts, and hopefully devise a strategy. I wished things were as simple as Zuri saw them. Just go down there, knock on the door and say, "Hi, we're here with the chuck wagon." Try doing that when people are already counting their biscuits.

We need something more than that to go with. We have to keep people off the ship until we know who to trust. Hell, I don't think I trust myself. The way I see it, fate is calling the shots, I'm just trying to score.

I can't believe Zack is being so negative. After what humanity has suffered, how can we hold anything but sympathy for each other? The colonists probably lost contact with their home base within the first eight minutes. They must be going crazy. I am, and I know we have supplies for generations.

But why haven't they acknowledged our calls? That is the million-dollar question with a one dollar answer. The colonists must have turned off their radios, because when we scanned earthward all we picked up was static haze. Right after the Exchange, the amount of radiation was conclusive.

The only other logical explanation is that they left.

Zack told me that cargo ships, a mile in length, cruise the inner space-ways. People can live very comfortably inside some of those freighters. They are more than huge barges; the ships are self-sufficient factories of food, fuel, and assorted materials. There are more travelling between Earth and Titan that keep the fueling operations going than those going to Mars, because of the long transit times. If the colonists can capture some of those, they will be set for life. But sitting around guessing is getting us nowhere.

Finally, we finished scanning the complex, and as I half-expected, there was no sign of life. Certain systems were malfunctioning, as per Pegasus' readings. For example, the air pumps were operating on backup controls. The colony's generated load was only thirty percent of the five-gigawatts they normally produced. I did not feel good about Mars at all, so I told Zuri to monitor me from Pegasus. I planned to go down armed and alone.

Zuri would not hear of it.

I knew she would never stay behind and we did not have the rest of our lives to debate. We went down together, and armed. We programmed the bot to bring Pegasus down to low orbit if we did not contact it within twenty-four hours. We wanted it to appear that we were part of a crew.

In forty-eight hours, the bot was instructed to shut down the engines, thus allowing Pegasus to crash. Following the old, "If I can't have it, nobody will," philosophy.

Pegasus has no offensive weapons, nor defensive ones. Other than locking the doors, we have no way of keeping others off the ship. Two people with laser pistols cannot stop five-thousand desperate and stranded people from taking over. They could easily blow a hatch and gain entry once we were dead. This gave us three days to look around and get back.

"I plotted the shut-down so Pegasus will drop right on top of the colony. Just in case we are not received with good manners." I announced.

"I don't know, Zack," Zuri worried, "suppose something happens to us?"

"That is exactly why I am doing this, so nothing will happen."

The descent was as gentle as a row around the lake. As we entered the thin Martian atmosphere, our jump-jets locked onto the magnetic guides of the pad. We sailed down and into empty pad number three. I looked around the launch bay from the security of the cockpit.

The control room was well lit, vacant, and disturbing.

I patched into the station's intercom, "Attention. Attention. This is Zackary Tops of the U.S.I. Pegasus. Anybody, please respond."

I waited for the silence to end. It didn't. I think, in that moment, Zuri accepted Pegasus' findings, there was nobody here. I counted three Sleep Cruisers, the twin-engine type. They could carry eighty-five people in narcosis apiece, which was not enough. Besides, they left these behind and the bay was not big enough for another three.

Zuri surveyed everything particularly carefully. I sensed she shared my apprehensions.

The air was pure here, which was a good sign. We searched the other ships and the control room together with lasers in hand. I tried to pull some information from computers, but naturally, I needed a clearance code. Zuri systematically scanned the facility via the intercom.

"We should locate the colony's control center," I told her.

"What will we find there?"

"Hopefully, some answers," I said optimistically. "It is obvious they did not leave on their own ships. If we can cut into the security system, we can view all their video cubes."

"Then, it is onto the control center," Zuri said with a touch of humor.

We arrived at the main airlock to the mining colony in the middle of the tube. It had been locked and secured from the inside. We had to cut the bolts with lasers. After several minutes, our pistols did the job.

While pushing open the massive doors, we were floored by the incredible stench that rolled out. Instantly, our questions were answered, the mystery solved; death was the cause of their silence. We grappled for our air masks, quickly slipping them over our faces to blot out the awful smell. A few deep breaths cleared my lungs of the odor, but it still lingered in my mind.

I saw Zuri on her knees, her body heaving; she was rocked by the emotional shock.

'This time I will be there for her,' I told myself. "It's alright,' I said as I placed a hand on her shoulder. 'But don't let it get you down. Perhaps some of the people survived. Escaped."

Zuri's tear-stained face shone painfully bright under the yellow warning lights we had tripped.

I did not know what horrors to expect next, and I was betting there were quite a few still to come. I wanted to send Zuri back to Pegasus, but not like this. I held her close as we drove along the corridor to the Main Dome. In that building was the security office. I knew the colony was equipped with more than a thousand audio/video recorders, so whatever happened here would be stored in the crystal cubes in the office.

Our car crept along at thirty miles an hour, its electric motor whining from the strain. It was a solemn drive.

Meantime, I knew I had to keep Zuri thinking positively, didn't want her to return to a mood of despair. "We have to find out what is wrong with the circulators. Purge this foul air and bring the colony back up."

"What the hell for?" she snapped, "There is nobody here now. They are dead, all dead."

"Maybe not," I was forcing myself to sound encouraging, "some could have evacuated. We will determine what the facts are first. Besides, others might be heading for this outpost, we should do what we can to make it livable. The scanners did not detect any structural damage, so we could be dealing with a mechanical failure.

But even if it is a computer malfunction, we can handle it. Pegasus has many spare parts and a complete synthesizing factory." My words echoed from the emptiness of the burnt corridor walls.

I did not know if Zuri was aware of the signs of gunfights all around us. In some places, the fighting must have been intense. Steel airlock doors, three-feet thick, lay melted and bent in access halls. But as we entered the control building, the destruction was all too evident and rampant. Machinery was blown apart; a fire had ravaged the two lower levels. I stepped out of the car and the floor crunched from the broken glass.

Zuri sat motionless.

I kicked over a metal sheet, and right there laid charred, barely identifiable human remains. *'The fighting that went on here must have been hellish,'* I thought.

I crossed the room to the stairs, and looked back once more at Zuri. I had better make this fast, not only was she in bad shape, but we were getting low on oxygen too. The place was dark, except for a few emergency lights that still burned. Most of the doors had been blasted open and that made it impossible to figure out which room I was in. Every area was the same, floors covered with debris, equipment smashed and burnt, and the badly decomposing bodies of the colonists scattered about.

Around the sixth level, I was sick of the scene, but as I turned back to the stairs, I spied a single door still intact. I drew my laser and shuffled through the mess.

The sign under the pale-yellow light read: RECORDS.

Thank God, because I couldn't stomach this place any longer. The door slid open to reveal a starkly different environment. It was bright, clean, and totally untouched by the madness that engulfed the rest of the building. The recorders were still running. I surmised this room had its own power supply.

I radioed Zuri. "I found it."

She mumbled something unintelligible back to me and I decided to get her out of there immediately, we had both had enough.

We spent the next week on Pegasus, while I sent the bots down to make repairs and vaporize the corpses. We monitored their progress from low orbit. Most of that time, we spent in the habitats making love. But truthfully, I could not wait to get back to the surface. And as soon as the bots bypassed the security lockout of the computer system, I was on my way.

Morbid curiosity fueled my jump-jet. I had to know what had ignited the fighting that took five thousand lives. The WestPac Mining Co. was staffed by people from West European countries, and all were tight allies. They could not have fought over any political fallout from the Exchange.

The Mars colony was not built like those of Earth, as it was not meant to be a long-term habitat. The miners worked a five-year contract then returned home. Thus, there was never a plan to build any food producing modules. With a two-year supply and only a four-month turn around, the outpost could survive any disaster short of a killer asteroid strike. Essentially, it was built to strip-mine the planet.

Spiders could synthesis compounds, but they needed raw materials to work, and one of the minerals most needed to feed the ever-growing twenty-first century lifestyle was iron. It was indispensable for just about everything; from hulls and walls to the cores of magnetic-graviton machines that made life in space possible. Mars did not have much else, but there was an abundance of iron.

WestPac Mining Company found it more cost-effective to peel away the planet rather than go chasing after asteroids, as the US and China did. They also located secondary resources that further reduced operating costs; ammonia, sodium, potassium, chloride, and magnesium, all chemicals necessary for solid rocket fuel. And although the amount of ammonia found in the soil was sufficient for producing fertilizers, the lack of water and other carbon compounds made it more useful as energy.

Producing iron ore in the form of fine red sand and processing the fuel to launch cargo back to Earth was what the settlement was built for, nothing else. It was extremely efficient because little else was built into the facilities. WestPac was not in the business of promoting comfort or longevity, and at the end of their five years, everyone was glad to go home.

To save time, I reviewed Director Felipe Marcal's log, starting with the day of the Exchange. Zuri's guess was right, they knew about Earth almost immediately. First, they lost normal contact, then switched over to remote transmitters located in space. I learned that the radio waves were jammed with pleas for restraint and sanity. The pleas went unheeded.

I thought the destruction of Earth was the result of the super powers and their nuclear arsenal, but that was only a small part of it. The communiques told the complete story. Seven cities were simultaneously attacked with nukes, New York, Los Angeles, London, Paris, Shanghai, Saint Petersburg, and Mumbai. It was transparent that whomever launched the initial attack did not target the capitals, they wanted the nuclear super powers to retaliate. As anticipated, they did, which is what we witnessed from Pegasus. However, the greater destruction was brought on by the "poor man's nuke"—railgun weapons.

The electromagnetic railgun can be land-based or carried on ships and launch projectiles weighting a ton at speeds twenty times that of sound. The projectiles carry no explosive, they are solid metal kinetic energy weapons which become hype-thermic in flight. They are sent on a suborbital trajectory to strike a city with all the force of a nuclear warhead, but none of the radioactive fallout.

Colombia built several in the mountains after their war with the United States. Argentina and Peru did likewise, and all the countries of the Middle East employed them. The shell was guided and nearly unstoppable, only the pulse laser cannons of the space stations could destroy them. The laser pulse heated the metal alloy causing them to break apart before reaching their targets.

Thus, destroying the guns was the best plan of action. An EMP caused by a nuclear detonation rendered the guns useless since they were electromagnetic weapons. Russia and the United States used both railguns and nuclear ICBMs.

Unfortunately, the Director was a better administrator than a commander, but at least been wise enough to withhold the information for eight hours. However, the secret leaked out when the normal communication channels remained blank and the probing questions started. Felipe Marcal called for an emergency meeting of the council as the radiation spectrum climbed.

The thirty-two members of the council represented the management and unions which regulated the populace. They watched and listened to the tattered transmissions singing Earth's swan song. Mostly, they were taped broadcasts; the last live transmission ended ten hours after the Exchange.

Almost instantly and unanimously, the council split into three factions. One suggested a calm 'business as usual' attitude until a long-range plan was devised. Naturally, this was the group Felipe favored. The next thought an immediate return to Earth was their only choice for survival. This was impractical, they did not have enough spaceships for everyone. Plus, there was no Earth to speak of, to return to. And last, there were those who said to not waste the two-year food supply on such a foolhardy and pointless mission. Led by Alexander Menninger, they felt they should rather begin converting the facility into a self-sustaining operation.

A compromise by the three groups would have been best. Instead, the lack of leadership by Marcal, doomed them from the start. I could tell right away he did not possess what it took to be a leader. His slumped shoulders and perpetually bowed head told of a man who had always been just a puppet figure. A man whose only authority was a signature.

Alexander Menninger, on the other hand, had a dynamic personality. His voice reverberated in the tiny confines of the security office. His presence was charismatic, even on video. Alex's plan was adopted by the colonists three to one. Only those who wished to return to Earth opposed his ideas. Mainly, they were scared and could not believe the destruction was so complete.

Joseph Stilwell was one of them; he rose to be their leader, and the most defiant. "This is a foolish waste of time. We need to send a scout ship, at the very least, to assess the situation."

"Assess the situation," railed Menninger, "we just listened to hours of transmissions and viewed the destruction of it. What's more, anyone left alive there will be in no condition to aid us. Accept it, Earth is dead. And if you don't want to join them then we need to retool these facilities."

"I think we can afford to send one ship," demanded Stilwell. "One ship can salvage vital equipment and food supplies, even if all the people are dead. What do you think, Marcal?"

"Well, it is not at all unreasonable…"

"Reasonable or not, it was put to a vote and we will start the conversion program. And wasting fuel and manpower is not going to get it done." Menninger gave Stilwell a scowl and shook his head in disbelief at Marcal. He left the control room and the two men in disgust.

As difficult as it was, they pressed on with the conversion. There were three main obstacles to Alex's plan. First was the hardware. The plant was designed to produce a high grade solid rocket fuel and iron compounds for hulls and gravitons; there was just one processing building for hydroponics. That building produced the air supply the colony needed, and its plants were unpalatable. Alex decided to remodel the refinery because the huge holding tanks were there.

The next problem, the part of the plan Stilwell hammered away at, they had very little edible vegetation in the colony. Most of the shrubbery the colonists maintained in their gardens was the flowering type. They planted for beauty, not survival. Only ten families had vegetable gardens; naturally, they were very protective of them.

The third factor was time. Could they grow a large enough crop to feed five thousand people in only two years? Even more important, could he instill confidence in their survival before then? It was a touch and go situation.

Alex was the chief chemical engineer, but he was not God. He had little raw materials to work with, so he improvised, breaking down the fuel they had produced and getting some of the necessary elements from the Martian soil. He knew only too well that one failure would bring down the whole colony.

"I looked at the latest reports," Stilwell sneered. "The rate of converting rocket fuel to a viable medium for planting is less than an acre a year."

"But in two years, two acres of food-producing farming paddies will provide enough crops to keep us alive for another year. Then we will have three acres and a surplus," Alex softened his tone. He was growing tired of the constant bickering of Stilwell and his followers. He was counting on success to win over the last of the holdouts. "It may be a slim margin at first, but if we can get through the two years without a major failure, we'll be home free."

"Home is four months that way!" Stilwell pointed to the sky. "By now, the colonies will be back online, food and supplies will be plentiful. I'm not saying we should go all the way to Earth," his voice was smooth and soothing, "and the WestPac Mining Company is probably a thing of the past. Sure, they are gone, but what about the others? What I'm saying is, we don't have to do this thing all by ourselves. We should at least give it a try."

"That sounds like a good backup plan, Alex. We send one ship to make contact with the colonies, let them know we have plenty of room here. If we could get one of the Agricultural colonies to come, or send a pod," Marcal had become the go-between for the two sides. He agreed with each man whole-heartedly. "Stilwell isn't asking for a lot. We don't need to send one of the cargo haulers, we send one of the sleepers, not much fuel. We must have a backup plan in case anyway, as you say, we suffer a major failure."

Two months later, that failure occurred. A fire ripped through one of the processors. The precious hydroponic fluid was contaminated. The fire had been no accident; it was set by Stilwell's group. His rhetoric had convinced them Alex's project was going to strand them. "Menninger is going to leave us without any fuel or food."

Seven of the colonists were arrested and executed. A week later, Stilwell led three hundred men on a raid of the armory. Within a few hours, they were battling in the control center, as they tried to commandeer one of the cargo ships. Armed with pistols, rifles, and lasers they fought for two days, succeeding only in knocking out the colony's controls. Afterwards, everyone suffered a slow painful asphyxiation. None of the five thousand men, women, or children of the WestPac Mining Company ever left Mars.

As I viewed the final days, I kept repeating in my head, '*if only they had held on another week. Then they would have known help was on the way. They would have received my message.*'

CHAPTER EIGHT

"Do you know what has happened?" rejoiced Zuri.

"To the colonists?" I grieved, sure she still believed some had survived.

"No! Not that, I have been waiting for three days to tell you MY good news."

"News! Why didn't you radio..."

"Oh no, this I have to tell you in person. Face to face. I want to see your reaction." She was vivacious, hardly standing still, the news about to burst out of her. She shouted, "I am pregnant!"

For a very long time I could say nothing. It was great news, but by far, the last thing I expected. I forgot everything else and held onto her for an eternity. Thoughts came to mind of life in a joyous parade, my heart pounded vigorously with expectations. Today, in the landing bay, life had finally become bearable. I knew it was everlasting.

I saw our lives in a new light. Our searching had ended, the misery was truly over. It wasn't as if we never talked about children since that awful day, we just didn't think it would make a difference. But it did, there was a change we could see and feel in both of us.

The change was not a momentary high, to come crashing down with the next storm. It wasn't something we experienced on the outside. It dug deep into our hearts, minds, and souls. Converting them with love and filling us with eternal hope. In the landing bay, we married, without words or witnesses. We became one, a single purpose, a unified identity.

Zuri told me she found out a few hours after I left for the colony. Medscan confirmed her suspicions; the sickness she felt at the colony was not shock or gravity bends. She was six weeks pregnant.

Medscan showed no DNA defects. We had nothing to worry about; the medical labs were fully automated, delivering a baby was a simple program. She was provided with the correct supplements. The baby's development was monitored, non-evasively. And when the time comes, the birth cradle's computers will control muscle functions to painlessly manipulate birth. Doctors are no longer needed for something as simple as childbirth.

Although we were anxious to know what gender it was, we did not request the information from the computer. Both of us agreed the baby deserved its privacy and dignity. It's a healthy baby, that is what's important now.

Zuri's pregnancy renewed my concerns about Mars.

While there, I had thought a lot about finishing Menninger's project. I figured everybody who needed a home would be flying here anyway. To that end, we were sending signals to our known-world every hour, expecting to reach a space station, and to offer hope. So far, we had received no replies; I assumed interference from the ionized cloud blocked the signals. It had spread some fifty thousand miles above the planet. And like some of the colonists must have done, I felt it was only a matter of time before a ship would emerge from the dust.

Reality was plain, it would take too many years to convert Mars into a viable environment. Primarily, it's in desperate need of water if it is to be a habitable planet. I proposed to Pegasus a plan to bring asteroids to Mars. Pegasus suggested sending spiders to the Belt to capture them. But having the spiders melt the asteroids to rain on the planet is futile, as the air is too dry and thin, and the water will simply vaporize back to space. Crashing asteroids onto the planet is the quick and dirty way of accomplishing the feat but Pegasus calculated that even a relatively soft bombardment into selective craters would destroy the colony. The planet might take decades or a century to recover. Not an acceptable outcome, we need a proper colony as soon as possible, say, within two to four years, so it can serve as a stopover between Earth and New Eden.

I used Pegasus' computers to refine Menninger's plan. With her superior manufacturing facilities and supplies, she can easily build the greenhouses. I wanted to release some of the livestock also, but Pegasus informed me that that would be impossible without human supervision. Zuri, on the other hand, wanted to reach New Eden as soon as possible. I had no intentions of permanently settling on Mars either, I merely wanted to give whoever had survived the Exchange a head-start.

The central problem was to supply enough air pressure to support a complex flora and fauna. The Martian atmosphere is nearly all carbon dioxide, in its infinitesimal quantity. Since air breathing animals had been restricted to small rodents and various insects, a deep hole compression chamber had to be dug. Even space spiders' laser-drills will take six months to core the planet two miles deep. To make matters worse, the solution we needed to grow the planktons and plantains, would take a year to produce.

It was not an easy task convincing Zuri to wait two years.

I reasoned with her, "If we leave now, the baby will be born in deep space. And when we reach New Eden he will still be a toddler. On the other hand, if we complete the project first, he will be at least five or more when we arrive. I think he…"

"She!" Zuri interjected. "She will be five or six."

"I guess that means we finish the Menninger Project?"

She smiled. "If I can have a girl."

"I think we should have discussed this earlier."

"And I think I will continue trying to contact Earth," Zuri said, hoping.

"Maybe we can launch a few probes into the cloud." I suggested, "If we analyze it, we might find a frequency to transmit on."

"I would try hitting someone with a probe," she chuckled. But it wasn't a bad idea.

The Menninger Project turned out to be more problematic than I anticipated. Not only was the Martian air too thin, but the water content of the soil was non-sufficient either. Trying to boil enough water out of its soil would take years of deep heated well drilling, I learned from Pegasus.

The colony was deliberately located a few hundred miles south of the equator in a large crater basin, an ideal location for solid fuel production. Arid conditions and abundant minerals from the meteor-crash eons ago were what they sought. To transform it from a chemical plant to an agricultural facility meant finding a good supply of water, in any form. I thought whimsically about Lowell's Canals.

But canals would take forever to dig and would not be effective anyway, water would evaporate long before reaching the colony from lack of pressure. I had a great idea though, to vent the enormous Volcano Olympus Mons to the north, and drawing water vapors and carbon dioxide through pipes deep inside of Mars.

Venting volcanoes worked back on earth to alleviate the quakes which wrecked the United States' west coast. It also aided air pollution problems and reversed the growing greenhouse effect. By releasing water vapor into the atmosphere, they essentially washed the air clean.

Pegasus computed the new plan; a system of three compression chambers and five hundred miles of connecting pipes. It will take the spiders a full year to assimilate the network from the Martian soil. The toughest drilling site will be the base of Olympus itself. A thirty-foot-wide hole has to be bored one-hundred-and-fifty miles in, before a vertical shaft a half-mile wide can be dropped. And all of this through the hardest rock on Mars.

I reluctantly agreed to return to the colony with Zack after the final plan had been completed, but he needed me close at hand in case trouble arose with his suit. I had worn the suit as part of my U.S.I.'s basic training, although I never did any work in one of them. So my whole training period consisted of two hours, just the fundamentals on how to put one on in case of an emergency evacuation. I had never needed to do so again. Now, if his suit locked up on him, I would have to find him and bring him back.

I worried about the baby and my growing stomach, but Zack proved that the two of us could easily fit in one hard suit. We sat comfortably on the torso ring while he explained its control settings. Even though the suit follows the wearer's every move—the soft inner suit is connected to the outer hard shell by a series of wire coils—one can operate the chest-plate computer by pulling the hands in and using the touchscreen controls. Zack walked me around Pegasus for a week before letting me go solo. But I did not want to spend a long time in the colony. The madness that had occurred there genuinely bothered me.

Zack and I went driving in the Martian summer afternoon to set up the drilling sites. The morning frost had disappeared by the time we set out in the magnetic propulsion car. We bobbed over the rusty iron desert on the shock waves from a particle accelerator, which is basically a large round dish topped by a black dome to screen out the ultraviolet light. We sped along at a hundred miles an hour to the first site.

When I stepped out, blue sparks jumped from my boots. The reaction is caused by iron oxides in the soil and electromagnets in the boots. It is a magical place, like nothing I could envision, with a pink sky and deep red sun overhead. Packed rosy dust swirled gently between my footsteps. The ground was littered with beer can-sized rocks everywhere and all of it in shades of crimson.

Before joining U.S.I., I had never been to the other worlds, as we referred to the colonies back on earth. Colony 5 was very exotic. Its zero gravity playgrounds and floating gardens astounded me. Yet, nothing compared to standing amid this strange backdrop and looking back at the shimmering black domes of WestPac. It amazed and at the same time terrified me like a picture of Hell. The only thing missing was the erupting flames. Even out here, I could feel the presence of the tortured souls drifting across this hopeless, lifeless limbo.

It's July 20, 2057. On this historic day, eighty-one years ago, Viking 1 landed on this planet. And today, we began operations at our second site. I used the occasion to study the frigid summer day. The temperature climbed to the mid-fifties; yet, the ground remained packed like tundra.

Zack aligned the monstrous black machine known as a spider.

It rolls on two treadmills that jut out from the base. Around its circular drum are the long slender silver tubes which produce the laser heat. From the top of the cylinder the hydraulic arms protrude. It was to these arms he connected six modules. Magic baby makers, he called them. They will fill up with the vaporized rock from the tunneling. Tied to an anchor line, they are free to fly about in the soft Martian breeze, like balloons at a carnival booth. I will enjoy coming out here to retrieve the hundreds of blue, green, and yellow balls dancing in the beautiful evening sky.

By that time, Zack assured me, we will have returned to Pegasus for good.

He loaded the modules with two-hundred, forty-feet wide, thermoplastic bags. When we do return, the spider will have crawled deep down a fifty-foot steel access tunnel. On the surface, the six modules will hold their lofty balloons; it should be a pretty sight.

Our final drilling site was in the great canyon region called the Valles Marineris. We descended through a thick blanket of mist, ice particles scratched at our bubble at about nineteen thousand feet. A thousand more and our car was imbedded in the sands. It was a finely ground powder that made movement difficult. I waded through up to my waist, even though my magnetic boots were set to high antigravity.

Zack said the dust was probably absorbing the suit's energy. Once the battery goes dead, we will sink as if we are trying to walk on water. He was managing to keep the spider in reach by running the tractors and using its arms as jets. There will be no retrievals made from this place. The real trouble here will be keeping the spider level in the shifting sand. Zack was hopeful that the spider would hit solid ground before long.

Confirmation of the spider's location was further hampered by the mist between it and Pegasus. It seems there was just enough iron in the ice to break up the signal. But once Pegasus initiates contact, the spider will reveal its views of the canyon and she will have a permanent reference point to zero in on.

The winds in the canyons are stronger than at the surface. The thirty-miles an hour gale isn't too difficult to see through, but it produces the sound of a million microscopic particles beating on my head like rain. It's a very dry rain here on Mars.

At last the spiders were ready to go and I tied in the remote sensor systems at WestPac Control Center to Pegasus. From startup and until the spiders have dug down a hundred-feet, I will monitor operations from the safety of the ship. Mars will become rather tumultuous once the searing laser heat, which will be absorbed by the carbon dioxide atmosphere, explodes into a fierce planet-wide dust storm. A cloud approximately a mile thick and several days long, driven by hurricane force winds, will roam the planet for the rest of the Martian summer. I hope I can still find the colony when it's over.

Along the crater rim runs a high-energy laser to vaporize the falling dust. It has enough power to disintegrate a ten-ton asteroid, like the one that formed this crater. But I expect the pressure to go way up; I just pray the system holds up. We can't come back until it's over, and I suspect we will lose contact when the storms begin.

"Are you feeling homesick, Zack?" Zuri was finishing the snaps on her flight suit.

"Just making sure we didn't forget anything, Honey. I don't want to leave the lights on; it will be one hell of a bill when we get back."

We climbed into our seats and the instrument panel's tiny green lights came on.

I looked momentarily at Zuri and smiled at the way her flight suit bulged. "Well, everything is secure."

"Everything OK with me too. All hatches battened down, captain," she gave me a mock salute.

The moment of apprehension passed with a long sigh and we lifted off, ascending by magnetic acceleration with no problems. After we broke atmospheric containment, I kicked in the jump-jet's rockets.

We had left Pegasus in a mirror orbit with Phobos, Mars' inner moon. Although she is larger than the moon, we felt that orbiting them within a few miles of each other would help hide her position. We did not need unnecessary surprises.

I returned my attention to the job at hand; a tricky head-on docking with the rapidly approaching ship.

Zuri reached for my hand as the black hole beneath Pegasus' neck loomed closer.

She was majestic with her head held high and wings flared back. The landing bay illuminated on my command; green arc lights rimmed the opening, forming a lane within the ship. The crosshairs on my radar scope fell a little to the left of the bay's center. I fired a short blast from the starboard retro-rocket.

"I'm cutting the aft thrusters to half," I informed Zuri.

My eyes darted around quickly, everything looked the same as we approached. Just the way it should be. Finally, I shut down the rockets and we drifted beneath Pegasus' huge head, entering the bay clocking five-hundred miles an hour speed. The red marking lights rushed past the cockpit one every second.

"Beginning countdown to bow thruster firing," I announced. "Five, four, three, two, one, and mark."

A great hand pushed me down in my seat. The yellow flames of the retro-rockets obliterated my view. After a second or two, I felt the violent vibrations of the jump-jet's wheels bouncing on the bay floor. The bouncing was over as suddenly as it began and the bay returned to view.

I turned to Zuri, "We are home!"

"That landing was a little rough," she complained, "Obviously, you do not know how to treat a lady in my condition. I think I will go lie down for a while, OK?"

"Sure, baby, and I will come see how you feel as soon as I get things in order here."

Zuri exited the jump-jet via a compression tube that led to a transport car. Minutes later, when I went to check on her, she was resting comfortably in our living unit. She looked good, the landing had merely shaken her up a little. It was a relief, I in no way wanted to exert her. I told her to sleep as long as she needed, we would fire up the spiders when she was ready. No one was going anywhere.

It is exactly four months since the Exchange and there has been no sign of survivors. I fear the same madness that infected WestPac may have swept mankind into oblivion. Pegasus' recorders show no one has tried to radio us while we were on the surface. I'm hoping Phobos' shadow is responsible for blocking out incoming signals, and as soon as we move to a higher orbit the radio will sing out. I hope.

Zuri joined me on the bridge after we settled into a standard orbit.

We crossed our fingers for luck, and I directed. "Commence drilling program."

"Spiders activated. Confirmation, three units working at 100% efficiency," Pegasus responded.

"Let's see if the on-site cameras are operating normally," I said.

Zuri punched a square yellow button on the communications board and a picture of the first spider appeared on the forward screen; the image fluttering continuously from the white-hot laser emitted by the robot. A steamy red cloud rose from the crater bed as the camera surveyed its surrounding. Every ten seconds another perspective of the landscape was displayed while we monitored the site.

She depressed the next yellow-trimmed square, marked, "video circuit #2", in green letters. The huge screen changed to the spider on the plains. We watched as the camera flashed its series of photos. Again, the dominant red cloud bellowed from the underside of the drilling machine.

The next panel in the row of ten was activated, and once more the same sequence of events occurred. All was normal.

She shut down the monitor circuits and the overall view of Mars returned to the screen. "Why is there so much dust?"

"Well, for one thing, the spiders are putting out temperatures of two thousand degrees. But be glad we are not down there right now, because in an hour or so, a lot of the ice holding the dust to the surface will melt. That dirt will become so thick it will obscure the planet."

She grimaced; a reaction to the painful memory of Earth.

I pretended not to know what had caused it. "Are you OK? Is it the baby?"

"No, I'm fine," she said with a smile.

"The dust should settle by the end of the Martian summer," I said elated. "About six months from now."

I watched the growing storm advance toward WestPac directly below. Zuri watched for a few minutes, then excused herself to prepare dinner. Within the hour, the storm completely blanketed the southern hemisphere.

Dinner was relatively quiet that evening. Zuri told me about some books she had been reading on natural childbirth. I told her the birth cradle didn't look very natural to me.

Life became routine since we returned to Pegasus. We spent most of it on the bridge monitoring either the spiders' progress, when a signal managed to break through, or the earthbound probes. In either case, there was little happening to excite us. In the afternoon, we went swimming, as it was good exercise for Zuri.

I am the typical expectant father, I'm ashamed to say. Every wince from her panics me. It feels as if I will never survive the next six months. I'm quite positive, that by the time the baby is born I will look like Zuri's father, white-haired and wrinkled.

Every night we go through our list of names. And every night, we end up with the same pair, Andre after her father, or Jennifer after my mother. Just before I go to sleep each night, usually after she is asleep, I kiss her belly softly and whisper to our unborn child, "I love you."

CHAPTER NINE

I passed into my second trimester without any complications; according to Medscan. I also found, since our return, Pegasus to be entirely too still and I could not spend enough time in the habitats. Finally, I turned off most of the inhibitors, except for the lions and such, giving free roam to all the other creatures.

Zack loved the atmosphere it created, a bit like Noah's Ark. He did however caution me to keep the farming decks restricted. But I didn't believe they would go foraging there, food is plentiful in their own habitats. The animals have been conditioned to living this way far too long to change now. Nonetheless, I left those decks' barriers' in place. Our little animal friends now explore the rest of their worlds but always find their way back to their sleeping nests at night.

It's a remarkable change for Pegasus. She is teaming with life, vibrantly active from end to end. She is whole, just as a world should be, not fragmented, but growing and entwining man, machine, and nature. Everywhere within her there is movement, and nature's music. The teacher told me the systems were safe from any burrowing insects or animals since they were encased in crystalized metal. The carpeting is self-cleaning, its fibers vibrate at an incredible speed beneath the outer layer, shaking dirt down to be whisked away in a powerful vacuum tube.

The menagerie atmosphere changed Zack too. Gone was his desire to hunt, fish, and conquer nature. I think he discovered the true value of technology; to bring together God and Man. A white rabbit he named Alice—after a song from the 60's Love Generation—started following him everywhere. And he made sure he was never without his cereal for her. His look told of a peace he had never known before. I know, it appeared in me too.

I come to the bridge with my tablet under my arm these days. The slender, square, eight-inch machine and I have become accustomed to going everywhere together. Into its memory chips I downloaded every library entry on child care Pegasus had to offer. There were so many things I did not know, unlike Zack, whose brothers and sisters undoubtedly made him an expert. My former experiences leave me totally inadequate.

It has been two months since we launched the probes; they transmit pictures and data about Earth from thirty thousand miles beyond the Moon.

"At this range, we are starting to receive quality information," Zack said.

The first detailed pictures of the cloud, which smothered the planet, were exactly as we expected; a light gray mass shimmered in the sunshine from its ice particles. Radar waves showed it was denser than a gaseous body should be, as the highly-energized cloud formed a cocoon around the planet.

Radar confirmed solid bodies within the five-thousand-mile space stew, but we couldn't get clear images of the structures, and more importantly, Zack could not pick up any standard energy fields. The whole area pulsated on random levels, we could discern very little about Earth. But by comparing changes in the cloud system at different intervals, we pieced together the likely existing conditions six months after the Exchange.

Since then, the planet had undeniably sped up its rotation by two hours. There were three regions emitting tremendous levels of heat, two in the northern hemisphere and one in the south. And they were still pumping ash into the clouds, some fifty thousand miles away. I assumed the size of the impact areas were missile strikes, as they covered close to five hundred square miles each. But Zack said some could have been RGPs, and he replayed a transmission out of Chile reporting the Andes Mountain range had crumbled due to Rail Gun Projectile impacts. Earthquakes and landslides sent a vast portion of South America's west coast into the Pacific. Beyond this, we knew nothing else. And somehow, Zack still had faith that the stations had survived, not only physically, but operationally as well.

He finally confided in me, "I saw Colony 5 receive a couple of hard hits as we left... But I'm confident they could have made repairs by this time. The fact that we picked up structures in the mass is reason to be hopeful."

I pressed the recall button at the bottom of the tablet; its screen displayed the last page I was reading. I nestled comfortably in the captain's chair. I could hear an occasional "humph" from Zack hunched over the sensor displays. He spent hours studying data from Earth and Mars, while I studied babies.

Zack called out twice. I had been rather absorbed in the new information.

"I thought you might want to watch as the first probe makes contact with the cloud." He said.

"Yeah, I guess so," I replied half-heartedly. "How long before it pierces the surface?"

"Oh, five minutes," he estimated, "it still has approximately twelve thousand miles to go. These last few days have revealed some interesting characteristics of the cloud."

"Really, like what?" I rubbed my stomach and balanced myself by Zack's shoulder.

"Is he kicking you?"

"Yeah, he's interested too."

"OK, first of all, the cloud seems to be shrinking. I'm not sure but that could mean that the ash and ice particles are getting heavier and falling back to Earth."

He waited for a smile, but obviously, I didn't realize the importance of what he said. The truth was, it was not the major discovery he imagined.

He continued. "Maybe this will make you happy. Look at this display on the big screen."

A red blob appeared at the front of the ship. Pegasus showed a picture that looked identical to the Martian dust storm below.

"This is an infrared view of Earth," he stated. "If you look hard enough, you can see faint lines running horizontally. They are regularly spaced," a self-assured gaze filled his face. "I think they are from an energy field operating within the cloud."

Zack held my hand as he counted off the final seconds. Then as he reached zero, the screen went blank.

"What happened now?"

"Either the probe destructed on impact, or more likely, the ions are jamming the signals."

"Then… That's it? That is all it can tell us?" I was disappointed.

"I took the ionization into consideration when I designed the probes. So for a while longer, the second one will pick up its laser transmissions from inside the cloud. I'll search in the mass by putting the number two probe in synchronous orbit. It will relay the information to us."

I was marking my steel messenger's telemetry when Zuri slid into the chair with me.

"How long will Number One be able to transmit data?"

"It's equipped with an ion battery so it should be able to recharge its power from the cloud itself." I hesitated to ponder other possibilities. "I guess it will operate until its sensors become caked with ash, on one hand, or it collides with a solid body on the other. There is a chance that the probe will get through that stuff and crash on Earth."

Her hand tenderly revolved on her bulging midsection "So how long?"

"Maybe a couple of months," then I added, "Maybe after I receive some data from Number One, I'll see if I can work out a way to navigate the probe. It will be another three days until Number Two is in place." I gently touched her stomach. Her jumpsuit was skin tight and showed a small lump sliding across her waist. "I think Junior wants to play with it too."

"He'll have to wait," she scowled playfully, "at least another three months."

"That soon," I couldn't hold back a smile.

Her figure was full and radiant, the stretch jumper hid nothing. The Jumper was made of silky smooth optic fibers, which allowed the wearer to change its color and patterns. Zuri chose variations of black and red, because, she said, they were kinder to her shape. But no matter what color her attire, there was no hiding the blush to her cheeks or the sparkle in her eyes. This child has been her salvation. And mine.

I work with real purpose in mind, having a desire to accomplish something that will last, and will serve the future of mankind. I have faith there will be a future. There must be other babies being born, we know that now. So, I work every day, sometimes in the engineering lab, but more often at the monitors on the bridge.

Using Probe Two as its guide, Number One navigated through the fog. It relayed data about the stations that were destroyed. There were also an alarming number of derelict spaceships. But the deeper it went, the stronger the radiation grew. I kept watching and hoping for a sign of life onboard a vessel.

There has been big trouble today. Pegasus picked up a major collapse in the canyon region. I can't evaluate from pictures on a screen so I must make an onsite assessment of the spider's condition. Zuri will want to go with me, but there is no chance of that with that angry storm out there. Although it is Zuri's anger I fear more, she will have to sit this one out.

After some back and forth debating I patiently explained that the heavy duty X-body Surface Rover will take a bad beating as it descends, which can be harmful to the baby, or her. Finally, I promised to return within seventy-two hours, job done or undone, and she reluctantly let me go.

The Surface Rover is a thirty-ton block with four directional rockets mounted on boons from its corners. Its main purpose is to penetrate dense or turbulent atmospheres and fly along at ground level. Because of my inexperience with such a vehicle, the trip could very well be a disaster. The rolling and yawing would rough her up, even in a pressure suit.

"But don't worry, I'll handle it fine," I kissed her. "And I promise to wear the pressure suit both ways. OK?"

She shut the airlock and headed for the launch bridge over the bay doors.

I unsnapped the pouch on the chair's headrest, where the pressure suit is contained, as it is part of the chair; I unrolled it then activated the air pressure. It ballooned to an opaque human form. *'Not exactly my size,'* I noted. I slid one hand across its chest until my fingers disappeared. Pulling the suit open with both hands released a blast of artic air.

Shivering in the suit, I saw Zuri through the floor glass panels of the launch bridge. On the level above there are windows to look in and out of Pegasus. I radioed her, "I'll send up a rocket, every twelve hours. Do you copy?"

"I should be going, do you copy?"

"No, you should not... Twelve hours. Alright?"

The suit is fully wired and transparent from the inside, a good thing, because I had to fly this duck, which has no auto controls. I grabbed the two handles and patted the floor pedals; it flies like a helicopter. The trick is to stay level and trying not to spin.

I maneuvered around the bay for a bit then pushed out. I could see Zuri clearly when I turned the ship about. She was pressed against the front window. I stepped on the pedals lightly and gently rocked the joysticks. The X-body waved goodbye and she waved back. A flash from the top of the arms and down I went.

I guided the ship north; thinking it would be best to descend directly into the canyon. I couldn't see through the dust to locate it, but that didn't bother me, a hundred-mile-wide hole is very visible to the radar. When I hit the atmosphere, I was no more than twenty-miles down range of the spider. "I'm going in," I radioed.

Buffeting started immediately, the winds changing directions erratically as I knifed through. But it wasn't the wind that rocked the X-body, it was the dust particles, some the size of skipping stones. I tried nosing down to get as much sail as possible from the ship, even trying to call out but the suit's air pressure choked off the words. The thumb buttons on the handles gave an extra boost to the bottom rockets, I strained, trying to keep the ship from flipping over; the worst scenario outcome. I was breathing all wrong in the suit too. Fear started creeping in; fear I would pass out if I didn't slow down. And just then, the X-body started spinning viciously around.

"One-hundred thousand feet," all good pilots learn to focus on the panel, not the chaos outside. But in this case, the view from the cockpit was of serene red clouds streaming past. Lights from the rockets were barely visible, just faint embers in the swirling smoke.

"Seventy-five thousand. Inhale slowly, exhale slowly, I must get under control," I told myself. Three G's… lucky Mars' gravity is so weak or I would already be out by now. I tried to yaw harder to my left. The green plane of the directional indicator slowed. I believe I hit another air current at forty-eight thousand feet. My descent slowed to a thousand feet per second and decelerating. "At three thousand. I am down to five hundred feet per second, steady, which is a safe breaking speed, Zuri." I hoped she heard my transmission.

Radar revealed I was forty miles from the south face of the canyon and five hundred above the surface. I had another twenty thousand feet to go to the canyon floor. The air was really calm at this altitude, which led me to believe it was hell in the canyon.

The Tharsis Region loomed ahead in the diminishing dust, its triple volcanic mountains reminding me of the Pyramids of Giza. It is their presence that acts as a windshield, allowing me to drop smoothly into the canyon's depths. Olympus Mons lurked as a ghostly shadow in the distance.

The winds picked up again, but at least they were in one direction, and what little light there was down here also faded. I navigated the ship through the dark bloody arteries of Mars. I followed my instruments, which were accurate to a couple of inches and that is close to perfect. I glanced at the laser detector, nothing yet. I will probably be on top of the spider's site before I can spot its beacon, that is how thick the dust is.

I eased back on my forward speed. The beacon pans the canyon wall to wall, but if I went too fast, I might miss the detector's yellow flash. Twenty-miles from it, I started to dive. I couldn't be far from it, unless, as I feared, I had been blown past the spot. Then again, I could always double back if I didn't come upon it soon. My biggest headache would be if the damn thing was inoperative. I might have to go out and search for the site on foot. But my choices were limited to next to zero if that was the case, my hard suit would lock up in seconds in this wind-driven dust, and a soft suit would be shredded.

He had only been gone a few minutes but I was already worried. As soon as his ship disappeared into the clouds, his transmission ended, although, a faint glow remained from the X-body's rockets. They soon vanished too.

I settled down to wait for the first rocket that would let me know he landed safely.

But as usual, and because he knows me well, Zack suggested I not sit in front of the panel and count the hours between signals. "Time will crawl if you keep vigil. Get busy, play with the animals, and I'll be back before you know it."

At twenty-two minutes past the hour, a rocket pierced the cloud cover. I calmly awaited his next one, which should come at about 6 p.m. I can't help it, I worry nonstop.

I recalled the next chapter on my tablet, but I couldn't concentrate. I found myself reading the same paragraph time and time again, driving myself into boredom. The baby began kicking, a warning that I was worrying too much. *'How could he leave me?'*

His assurances echoed in the emptiness, "I flew through Hell, and worst in the army."

'Zack is only on a return voyage.' I must calm myself down. And the baby agreed, by giving me another hard shot to the ribs.

I zigzagged in that canyon, retracing my path a dozen times before the indicator flashed. The massive landslide of rocks buried the spider's portal twenty-feet deep. The laser beam had bounced to the surface through the crevices. But it wasn't a hot beam, so it had no power to cut through the rock. I could only guess that a thermal buildup beneath the surface had caused the shearing of the canyon wall, the same way ice cracks when dropped into warm beverages.

Rocked by the wind, the X-body teetered on the boulders. I took out the hand laser and checked its charge; I needed to cut an access tunnel to the portal and hoped it didn't give way during the landslide. While I donned my hard suit the X-body's rockets blasted away the loose debris. A nagging thought wormed through my brain, what if another cave-in occurred while I dug; surely, I would be buried alive. If that was to be the case, I prayed I would be crushed like a beer can instantly, instead of waiting a month or more for the suit's power pack to drain. But the heat from the rockets should fuse the remaining rocks together, so a cave-in was unlikely.

'Poor Zuri,' I thought, seeing her in my mind alone and worrying, as she tends to, but feeling worse at the idea of something indeed happening to me.

I opened the bottom hatch and stepped out onto the smoldering ground. Thankfully, the massive feet of the X-body shielded me from the ferocious winds. I began vaporizing the rock, a blast then wait, another blast and wait. I knew it was going to take a long time.

The hand laser is a bulky basketball-sized globe with two big handle triggers on either side. It's a low power device, especially compared to even the smallest spiders, and I have to stop often to clean its lens. But it will clear an ample size hole for me to climb down. Luckily, the composition of Mars' soil is low density.

After some ten hours of blasting, I saw the first glimmer of the portal. The steel hatch appeared to be intact; but I still had to widen the base of the hole to inspect the entire door frame.

The heat of the rockets had completely dwindled away and my suit shimmered beneath the halogen landing light from the icy droplets which clung to me.

'That's enough for one day,' I thought, *'better get out of this soup can before it locks up.'*

My legs burned with fatigue as I climbed the ladder. Good thing gravity is so low or it's possible I would not have made it. I lowered a small spider down the hole; it will carve out the base overnight and I can open the portal first thing in the morning. I considered this mission a success already.

I was eating a three-course dehydrated meal when my watch started beeping. It's time to send up another rocket. God, how I wish I had let Zuri come along. We haven't slept apart since my savage rebellion, I was sure I was in for a long night of bad dreams.

It was pitch black outside the ship and my childhood phobia of the dark lurked just around the corner. I remember crying out to my mother that witches were hovering at the foot of my bed.

'Thank your Dad for all the Brimstone and Damnation speeches. Just what a five-year-old needs.' She would say.

The fear was so strong it stifled me, until my breath burst out in one long shriek. I learned quickly you never get over those kinds of fears, merely learn to live with them, always knowing it lies below the rational mind, waiting to choke you to death.

"I know you're not hearing this," I said, "but I had the radio channel open all day, and all I picked up was static. Damn dust..." I twisted in the chair, thumbed a lever to raise my legs to a more comfortable position and continued to the dead air, "Just polished off my beef stick and apple pie crackers. But nothing beats your home cooking, Honey, or you. I hate this low gravity life... Oh, no, not complaining... Hell, work is three times easier in this Netherworld."

The constant scratching of the dust and the never-ending howling wind outside the cockpit made it sound like a tornado wrapped in a blizzard.

"You thought it was cold and gloomy before? The snow that appeared and vanished is here to stay. Boot deep too. And it is damn dark, oh damn!"

The fact is, I can only see directly under the lights. The ground is entirely covered by dry ice again.

"There is a bright side. These spiders spin a tough web. I'll bet when I check the well and tank sections it's going to be as smooth as glass. I'm going to install a new beacon too, a close range hot cover beam around the long-range signal beam. That will make it hard to miss, not like searching for reflections in the rubble." I kept talking, babbling like the Martian wind. I don't recall when I finally fell asleep.

The captain's chair had suddenly become unmanageable. A couple of jolts in my stomach, and the uncontrollable urge to pee, woke me. Soft warm yellow sunlight sprayed across the bridge. I struggled to my feet. It is supposed to be easier having a baby now, but it is not any easier carrying them. It was 7 a.m. and I had missed Zack's signal. In fact, I missed last night's as well. I guess he was right about falling asleep waiting. I'll have to check Pegasus' records later. At this moment, I have a more urgent matter to attend to. I waddled off the bridge.

The ship's bell rang loud and long this morning. I decided to skip breakfast; I couldn't eat any more of that dry crap anyway. I suited up right away and was almost out of the ship when I remembered the signal. 0839 hours, Zuri would not worry yet, she knows I am a late sleeper. I watched it from the cockpit, a flaming tail wiggling through the crimson mire. Then I plodded off to the lower hatchway.

The winch and hook made a sharp screech as I pulled it over to the opening. I climbed into the wire cage and hit the red button. Down I went through the drill hole to the portal. The spider had done a good job down here; the control panel was clear, the ceiling high and firm. No chance of a second cave-in.

The control panel sat on a pole four-feet high on the edge of a ring of white lights. They marked the portal's rim. It had only two large buttons, one green and the other red, open and close. I stepped into the ring, pressed the green button with my gloved palm and was lowered down the access tube. A second ring of soft white lights glowed on the platform and I could see my reflection on the walls as a funny, squat, four-foot blue and yellow can with a round head. I took out a small ultrasonic device to measure the tube's dimensions. It will detect any flaws in the structure to a thousandth of an inch. So far everything was good.

Three red flashing LEDs formed a tiny triangle at the far end of the conduit. My headlamp illuminated the entire pipeline; the valve was closed as indicated. I heaved a heavy sigh and started off to the next section.

The valve was so far away that all I could see was the indicator and a starburst reflection from my lamp. According to the ultrasonic meter it was five hundred yards away. I wished I had a tri-cart right then. If there was damage to the system, I figured it would be in the tunnels near the surface. Still, with seventeen miles of them to check, I was not going to enjoy this.

My best bet was to go to one of the hub connections, open all the valves and check each tube from there. I pressed a button on my waist and the right thigh pocket slid open. "I don't need you right now," I said to the meter, dropping it into the hole in my leg. I hit the same button and the door closed. The nearest hub was a half-mile down this line.

I had stuffed myself at breakfast and was now paying the price. I lay stretched out on my side, one hand trying to soothe the baby, anxiety makes me eat. Nerves make me ache, and not being able to talk to Zack is making me very nervous. I asked Pegasus to relay a situation report to our unit. It informed me almost immediately that there had been two rockets launched, one the night before, and one at 0839 hours, March 12, 2058.

"He overslept again," I thought aloud.

It dawned on me then that we have been gone almost a year now. I can't say the time has passed quickly; it seems to move in spurts, fast at times and crawling at other intervals. At least while we are in orbit or on Mars, we have normal days and nights. It makes keeping track of time a little easier. I started thinking of Zack and the baby in the future… and soon drifted off to sleep again.

Finally, I reached the hub; it was high above the monitor facility between the three tanks. I went into the control room where I could see the top of the tanks. Two thirds of their bodies were buried in the Martian crust. Huge pipes rose hundreds of feet to intercept other pipelines. There were three six-arm hubs above me and five four-arm connections below.

I opened all the valves and returned to L.C.6. The ultrasonic released a long soundwave that should be cancelled out by the harmonics of the network. That is, if the system was still symmetric. The network has a low-pressure air supply. It aids the drying process to have some air in the pipes, and the soundwave would take a while to travel through the system.

The ultrasonic's green LED throbbed rhythmically as it fed dull tones into the air. I held the meter stiffly in my outstretched palm, knowing motion could destroy the readings. The tiny monitor showed a circle with red crosshairs, the same as a radar screen. Any flaws will show up on the display and its distance will easily be pinpointed.

"Oh, Hell!" I cried at the red dot in the outer edge of the third quadrant. "A defect." And just to be sure, I cleared the machine, placed it on the ground and ran the test again. Five minutes later, the dot flashed on the display like before.

Back in the control room I checked its position on the system's mapping board. It was a feeder line to tank number one that was causing the trouble. The section was another five miles lower in the lithosphere and about one hundred and forty miles north. That placed it deep in the Tharsis Bulge. That sector had been completed before the cave-in, but that does not mean it could not have caused the collapse.

I mumbled a few curses at my bad luck, then, checked the time, 1320 hours. After lunch, I will survey the damage and decide what to do. "Vocom open," I said to my suit.

"Ready," replied the microprocessor in my helmet.

"Start internal nourishment please," I told the computer.

"Commencing liquid nourishment program," the sultry voice responded. "What type of flavoring do you prefer?"

"Surprise me," I said sarcastically.

"Cherry flavoring added, you may begin intake through the mouthpiece."

"Vocom close."

A clear plastic straw popped up in front of my lips. I drew some of the cool liquid down my throat quickly, not realizing how dry I was and coughed a little from the unexpected coldness. *'Cherry,'*

When did a computer ever lie?

As I sipped on the juice, I glanced around the control room, and my eyes came to rest on the equipment room door. I opened it and there it was, shinning and inviting, a silver and white tri-cart. Those spiders really cover all the angles when they go to work. Not only did they build the entire facility, they also manufactured all the necessary support equipment. Thank God for a well-designed and thought out program.

The toolbox under the seat was loaded as expected. Amidst the various wrenches, meters, and spare electronic boards was a black eight-inch octagon box. I flipped it a foot above my head and let it tumble carelessly back into the compartment. I slammed the thin padded seat down on the inert spider.

I grabbed one of the handlebars and positioned my massive boots on either side of the control column. The tri-cart jerked forward when I pressed the starter button. I gave the trigger a lighter squeeze and rolled gently out the door.

The quickest route to the intake section is around the control deck and down the north elevator, the inlet pipes are at the bottom of the tanks, filling different chambers within the three tanks. They branch out under the Tharsis Bulge to tap into Olympus, Pavonis and Ascraeus Mons, three of the four volcanoes which dominate the territory.

Passing the decompression chambers, gusts from the mighty turbines almost toppled my vehicle. The blades are fifty-feet long and twenty-feet across. They need to be large, because when lava flows through the tanks, these giant fans force a million pounds of hot gases through the tubes every second. Some of those gases will be released directly into the atmosphere, others will be combined or compressed to form liquids. The lava will go from one chamber to the next, being decocted of its vital minerals, and finally pumped back into the Martian mantle.

At last the elevator reached my level; the pressure was almost at one atmosphere here in the bowels of Mars. I drove north along the access tunnel, looking for the closest manhole to the trouble spot. The area looked sturdy from the outside; I couldn't see any cracks in the pipe.

There was no evidence of a cave-in either, all the lights were aligned as straight as an arrow and there was not a speck of dirt or debris in the tunnel either. I was finding it hard to believe that the intake pipe could have been damaged, as the thinner walls of the access tunnel were not.

These intake pipe walls are twelve-feet thick heavy-duty steel webbing, so a more likely occurrence could be that a tremor jarred the spider off course, causing a weak spot within the wall. But I doubted the plausibility of this causing a catastrophe. These computers are too damn perfect and they expect everything else to be the same.

Green illuminators marked the ladder at section I-1C6, one-hundred yards from the firewall at the end of the access tunnel. Another five miles beyond the yellow and black striped barrier, the pipe dropped vertically into Mars' molten body. The interior of the planet here is still hot, but not like the spinning hot core of Earth; Mars' middle is cooler, like super-hot tar, made mostly of iron.

I climbed to the manhole platform on top of the pipe, the yellow letters on the control panel read, "work in progress." Well, maybe there was a problem after all, as the control room had this area as code green. I opened the manhole; I could probably fit the tri-cart down, if only it would drive up the ladder. That crazy idea passed and I climbed in.

It was sweltering inside and the glare blinding even with the filters on high power. Luckily, I did not have to go far. Meter in hand, I began another damn walkdown. It didn't take long to pick up the trouble either. The heat was interfering with the meter, I surmised, as it wouldn't give a steady location.

A momentary shadow crossed my line of vision. I threw the useless device aside and ran for the manhole.

Black and smoking, the bulky spider gained on me quickly. Its smoldering hide pushed me against the wall and its lanky steel arms sprayed a fine mist as it gracefully flew by. I had no chance. The deadly vapor of crystallized metal cut into my suit. Sparks sputtered around and systems failed, an alarm sounded quietly in my ear, and my upfront display turned red. Jesus Christ, I could not move!

"Pegasus," I requested, "status please?"

"The time is 1754 hours. All systems are functioning normally. All life forms are well and accounted for. No transmissions received. No observations to report…"

"OK. Stop." I flopped down into the captain's

chair.

Alice nudged my feet, she missed him too.

I wondered if Zack would send up a flare at six o'clock, sticking to the original time line, or at eight, twelve hours from his last signal. I hoped he would not keep me waiting. "He's probably finished and on a launch pad ready to go," I told myself.

I finally got my soft suit disengaged, so at least, I was free to move around in the shell, which was webbed solidly to the wall; the first sweep had caught my midsection. Since then, the spider had shorted out the hard shell and been turning it into a permanent part of the pipe. The steel was not hot enough to cut all the way through, thank God, but it was unbreakable.

The suit is only good for thirty-six hours on emergency power, and I have already used up six of them. My prospects didn't look good. Even if I cut myself out, I won't last long enough to reach the manhole, the inner suit will burn right off my back in this heat. All I can do is watch as the spider comes and goes, entombing me deeper each time its dark red eyes appear.

The hot web made a sizzle that rang through the hard suit. I've got to stay calm.

"Zuri will come when I don't signal her. The suit's distress signal will lead her right to me. Oh, God, what about the baby? Wait, she can land in a lighter craft under Pegasus' magnetic pulses. But then what? No… I have got to get at the radio panel."

I had to stop that errant spider and call another one to dissolve my bonds. And I had better do it quickly, because the longer I take, the more embedded I'll be.

How could I have been so stupid, entering an area with an active spider? I know better than that. Anyway, I

James L Hill
have got to get out of here, fast.

CHAPTER TEN

I waited. Eight o'clock passed. I watched the forward monitors intently and with growing impatience. By 9 a.m., I had not blinked, and there was no signal from Zack in twenty-four hours. I absolutely have to get myself down there, and Pegasus should be able to do it. I am no pilot, but with all the vehicles on board, there has to be one that all I have do is turn it on.

"Pegasus, consider a totally automated landing at WestPac immediately. This is a search and rescue mission by me."

"Working."

I paced the bridge. *'Damn it, Zack! I told you not to go. But it's no longer important. Now, I must just find a way to get to you,'* I watched eddies in the bloody clouds.

In a way, they looked invitingly warm and calm, the storm not appearing dangerous at all. But radar readings revealed a different story, wind gusts were between two hundred and two hundred and fifty miles per hour.

I have never flown anything, never even had to push the buttons, so I have to convince myself that it can't be too hard. The crafts I have seen Zack fly were not very complex.

He used to say, "They design them for chimps, the perfect pilots, someone who will push the button and not care about the dangers. And as it happens, that's me, I'm the chimp. I don't want to know how it works, and I definitely don't like spending much time in manuals, because it is better to learn in the seat."

'Oh, God! He used to say, things are never that desperate. But right now, I can feel they are.'

He could survive in a hard suit for a month, but I still need to get down there.

"A system has been devised," Pegasus replied after too-long a silence. "A magnetic drop capsule will provide adequate protection with minimum command requirements."

"What are the requirements?"

"The status of WestPac Mining Colony is unknown. If landing conditions are impossible, you must disengage the magnetic beam and fly to a safe site," informed Pegasus.

"What do you mean impossible?" I was afraid to ask.

"Worst case scenario, the laser field fails to disengage. Attempting to penetrate it will fatally damage the capsule."

"What are the difficulties of an alternate landing?" I asked. Just to know what I was getting into.

"Unable to calculate. Unknown surface conditions, unknown minimum altitude for parachute deployment, and unknown capabilities of pilot using manual rockets," replied Pegasus.

"Is that all," I said confidently, "prepare the system for launch."

While Pegasus prepared the capsule, I got out two hard suits. I doubted anything could penetrate one of these things or crush someone while inside, as they are like wearing a garbage can. The suit can stand on its own and you can sit down, curl up and sleep, or get in almost any position. Zack told me often enough that the worst thing that can happen is having the suit's servos freeze. Then, somebody will have to carry you back.

I didn't worry about landing at WestPac; it was

operating normally when we left. We had changed all the codes and I will begin transmitting them before liftoff. I am sure the laser field atop the crater protecting the landing pads will shut off when I get in range. It only needs to shut down for a second before I reach the opening.

Pegasus warned me that I could not contact her once I entered the cloud coverage. There could be no abort signal. That was irrelevant, I had no plans of returning without Zack.

I sat in one of the two seats and strapped in. The capsule was an extremely small double-headed bullet. Well, I wanted something I did not have to fly, and this thing did not look like it could. I patted the other hard suit next to me, "Don't worry now, and just leave the controls to me. I haven't lost one yet."

There was very little equipment on board. A few digital meters, two small control panels for turning on or off the magnetic coils and deploying the parachute in front of each chair, some radio gear, and four tanks behind the seats. The rocket controls were on the handgrips. It was a very compact ship.

"OK, Pegasus, I'm ready to go," I told the computer.

The displays lit up and the bay floor slid open. I descended through it, slowly at first, but I quickly picked up speed. The ship took an instant hard hit as it pierced the crimson atmosphere. I kept my eye on the lower portal for the ring of green lights that would tell me the laser field was off. A loud buzzer will warn me if it is still on, but I don't know when, or if it will be too late for the parachute. With a two-hundred mile an hour wind outside, deploying the parachute will clear me of the crater, but it won't slow my decent by much. The air is too thin for that, I will hit hard who-knows-where. And I dare not use the rockets.

Long yellow streaks of lightning rocked my capsule, each strike causing an ear-pounding thunder clap. All the metallic dust has made the storms extremely violent. I am going straight down with nothing in sight.

I searched for the laser beacons that marked the crater.

Unexpectedly, there were four shimmering blue pillars around me. The base was still hidden by the clouds, but I knew I was right over the launch area. The green ring appeared shortly afterwards and I sensed everything was perfect. The capsule touched down softly onto the pad.

'Why didn't Zack use this system? I could have been here from the beginning, and I'd know where he is now. We could have prevented whatever went wrong.'

The docking procedures took a few minutes, and then I was on my way to the control center. From there, I could locate Zack and call up a Caterpillar. Fear filled the corridors of the base like ghosts and I couldn't stop thinking that something more than terrible had happened.

Mars has long been known as the Cursed Planet. Many robotic missions had failed before Viking 1 landed safely. Then came the three manned missions, all ending in the loss of crews. WestPac had been the only successfully manned mission, but now, they too are gone.

'What if I get to the control center and find there was another cave-in?' I pictured Zack buried alive in his hard suit. Then, another picture jumped into my head, that of my father. He was walking through the grounds of the Central Ministry Building on television. *'No. Get out of my head. I don't want to see this. Not again.'*

The news anchor's voice was loud and distorted, "Minister Mlimo is on his way to the General Assembly meeting."

Crowds of people were milling around. *'Are they blind? Don't they see him? Right there on the steps. Assassin!'*

A single shot rang out and slowly faded.

The announcer's voice called to me, "Zuri, your father has just been murdered. Look! See him there, lying on the white marble steps with his blood flowing into his own Lake Retba. You are an orphan now, Zuri. You are all alone in this world."

'No. No. No. Not happening again. I couldn't save Daddy. But this time, I am here. I will save Zack.'

I watched the chronometer rolling off the elapsed time; it was getting closer to the end of the maximum battery life, and closer to the end of mine. Rewiring the radio was a wasted effort, too many of the suit's circuits had been damaged. And there was a short circuit draining the reserve power supply as well. There was nothing else I could do except wait. Zuri would surely find a way to rescue me. I kept telling myself she was on her way.

I figured she could not make the trip herself, but she would send a bot. I imagined an army of tiny spiders overpowering my nemesis. They would rip its legs off and its molten blood would trap the inferno beast. Zuri's minions would claw through its optics and eat its fusion heart. Then their little shiny smiling faces would greet me and chew through my bonds. I had to hold out until then. At the twenty-fourth hour, I shut down my suit. It will start up again when my air becomes too foul. I have to conserve energy. That is what I learned in a trauma bag…

The Yari River Zone Invasion turned out to be a catastrophe. The Colombians found out about our southern crossing and used tactical nuclear rockets to stop us. It took weeks before we were evacuated. I spent the time in a field medical unit, suffering from burns. I survived because I buried my unit in the mud and saved my power reserves.

The hours of intense pain were mine to endure as I

left my unit off. I remember the dull beating of the shells destroying other soldiers from my company. Their units betrayed their positions. They were like flares in the night to the electronic sweeps. Three thousand men lay dying in plastic bags on a forgotten field. My unit was still functioning when an independent relief team swept the site. The Colombians had eventually tired of shooting fish, or been driven off, or become busy elsewhere.

I have less than twelve hours on the clock but I know how to use them. The main problem is that each time the power comes on to refresh my air supply, it takes longer and requires more energy. There are also drugs in this suit, neural paralyzers, if I must use them, I will!

WestPac's control center showed Zack's exact location. It also informed me that he had been sprayed. The status of his hard suit was undeterminable. The last reading showed a total system failure.

I heard his voice echo in my head, "People who get sprayed are buried in their suits."

He never said why and I did not want to find out now.

The caterpillar was ready to roll out of the bay and it was not a cute little bug as its name implied. The tires alone were twelve-feet high and an elevator lifted me to the driver's compartment. Each of the ten freight cars rode on a pair of those mammoth wheels. Each pair of wheels was independently propelled to push and pull it over irregular terrain. Mars is not a flat place; there are endless miles of craters and dunes. The caterpillar is the only vehicle that can maneuver over them during the dust storm seasons.

I gave the map a cursory glance again. It was a five-mile journey, and most of it fighting a hundred miles an hour head-wind. The wind kicked the machine repeatedly as I rumbled out of the bay. I set the throttle at half way, and then nudged it a little further.

Visibility was bleak. The laser tracker, though, painted a perfect picture on the windshield. I held the big round wheel with both hands as I bounced along, my stomach only a precious inch from the black iron. I headed for a main access tunnel and from there I will take a tri-cart. I have no idea what I am looking for but the guidance computer is keeping me on course.

I rolled swiftly down the sides of the craters, dodged the dunes in the middle, and fought to climb out the opposite sides. The smaller ones I avoided completely, the huge smooth craters were the easiest to cross, and those deep flat ones were traps. I toppled the caterpillar trying to climb the steep sides of a flat-bottomed crater… I am lucky to be wearing a hard suit fastened to the seat and the inflated inner soft suit was like bubble wrap within the shell. Also, the caterpillar, with its independent body sections' ability to rotate three-hundred and sixty degrees, could right itself and keep on rolling.

I aimed for the straightest route possible. Communications between surface locations are great, since it's all underground and not affected by the weather. I already knew Zack was on emergency power, and there were only six hours of it left. I especially worried about his frame of mind. It had to be nerve-wracking watching time run out.

I recalled the reports from the South District cave-in of 2031, and the trauma the afflicted endured. I was beginning to wonder how much more could Zack take, or me. In 2031, diamond miners detonated their supplies after a week of entrapment. Records recovered after the tragedy disclosed how quickly people gave up hope. Without contact from the world above, the miners lost track of time, one day seeming like an eternity. A quick and painless death became an inviting alternative to the idea of slow starvation and agonizing dehydration.

It was a rough drive but I made it to the blockhouse. Bright green lights shone on its steel doors. They lowered, sucking in a huge amount of dust before me. My headlights revealed it to be a large empty cavern. The doors closed and sealed out the roar of the wind, but I couldn't rest yet, Zack was a long way from here. I broke out the tri-cart, the emergency case, and the hard suit into the passenger's seat. I climbed in and down the dimly lit tunnel we went with time running out.

It wasn't a direct route this time; I was taking the turns as fast as I could. I tumbled a couple of times, but no harm done, just time lost, precious seconds wasted re-loading. I got lost on a few curves and lost more time. I homed in on his signal, which grew fainter. I knew his location and had the path displayed before me, but my desperation blinded my teary eyes.

Thirty-six hours expired. I pushed faster. Would not give up. I couldn't quit, just hoping for a miracle or something that would not come to pass. Zack's tri-cart stood by the ladder with its warning lights blinking steadily. I grabbed the case and scaled the ladder as fast as I could. Thick yellow smoke rose from the opening and the control panel read, "safe to enter" in green letters. I had shut down the errant spider and sent it back to the base from the control room.

I started the small spiders and dropped them down the portal.

Once I reached the bottom, I saw Zack. His suit jutted from the wall, he was halfway embedded in the shiny steel. I peered through his face mask, refusing to believe the worst had happened.

The glass was dark and his face not visible behind it. The suit's functions had ceased. I quickly plugged the umbilical cord from the spare hard suit into his shoulder re-ceptacle. I hoped, no, prayed, I had arrived in time.

A mild cold humming breeze tickled the back of my neck. The air tasted good, too good, I choked on the chilly sweetness.

"Zack, you're alive!" The proclamation from Zuri was all I needed to hear.

With renewed vigor, I pulled myself up by the armholes, having no idea that my face appeared in the glass emaciated, darkened, and eyes bloody red.

"Zuri," I wheezed, "I've been waiting for you."

"I'm here now, Honey. Sit back, inhale slow and deep," she whispered with difficulty.

Relief echoed throughout the pipeline as I started crying. Tears of joy, thanks, and love, which I couldn't hold back, fell freely. Then I fell back against the other wall, to watch the spiders work.

Ten hand-sized Black Backs positioned themselves around his hard suit. Sparkling streamers flowed from their tails, building little dunes on the ground. The black mask stared at me, Zack's iron arms reaching out of the shimmering mist. I kicked a pile of dust and watched it rise again, and again. No matter how fast the spiders worked, they were too slow for me. I could not get him free down here, I could only dig him out. I remembered the colony has a heavy laser that will cut through the suit's locks.

Zack had not stood up again and uneasiness built within me as the minutes passed painfully slow. But his vital signs were good, I kept his condition on my face mask display. Fear that he might have suffered brain damage from the lack of oxygen gnawed at me.

The shower of fine steel dust grew fiercely. Harsh yellow light was everywhere, except for where Zack stood. Finally, he teetered forward and the blinding lasers ended. I held his hands for a second; although he was still encased, I could get him out of here now.

"Zack, are you ready to go back?" I called.

It had been eight hours and he had not made a sound.

He peeked at me as his head bobbed from side to side. "Honey, you do the driving," he joked.

"All strapped in."

He still looked drawn and languid, but not as bad as before, and gone was the deep red from his eyes. I studied him a little closer. "Are you alright?"

"I'm OK... Just have a bad headache and stiffness in my joints, ha ha ha."

"Let's go home." I said and revved the tri-cart.

The spare hard suit walked behind, carrying Zack still within the old mess. Then he told me how he managed to survive two hours past the limit.

"When I get out of this can, I'm going to let Max here, give me a kick in the butt… A really hard kick."

But he had to wait for that retribution. It took the colony's laser another four hours to cut all the electromagnetic locks.

I hooked his lifeline to the laser table and started the gun. A clear dome covered him, and then the laser's hazy white light filled the chamber.

Finally, I started to remove my own hard suit. Lifting the helmet, the cool dry air was a joy to feel once again. When I finally stepped down from the boots' platform, my legs were rubbery and I could barely stand. Being in the suit drained my strength; I knew exactly why Zack hated these things. It had sucked the life right out of me. I sat down to wait and fell asleep on the airbed in the pressure room.

The light show ended and the plastic dome rolled back into the table. The laser had split the suit down the middle and along both sides. I pushed and it clanged onto the floor. I arose from that sarcophagus, lucky to have Zuri, and glad to be alive. All my thoughts were of her, and the things we would do as a family. *'The First Family of New Eden, that's who we are!'*

I switched on her gravity inhibitor, even though I felt well enough to carry her without it, but in both our conditions, I would not risk dropping her. I swept her weightless body up and took her to the living quarters. She was in a deep sleep, and I imagined anxiety had to be bad for her and the baby, so sleep was the best medicine for her right now.

I was glad she didn't know how close I came to the end. The suit didn't have enough power to run for another hour. It was off when she found me and it probably would have stayed off if she hadn't. Lucky for me, the suit's thermos layer was not compromised, because the oven temperature inside the pipeline would have roasted me in the first hour. The next time I get in one, I am definitely taking Zuri along. I still had to evaluate the damage, but this time, I would do it from WestPac's control center.

Bad news was waiting for me there; dust had partially buried the colony. Zuri had forgotten to reactivate the field. I started up the laser and its green blanket unfurled, the atomized dirt making beautiful flowing wind patterns over the crater. But not much damage was done and I called a workforce of spiders to clean up. The primary site was the launch pad, that had been completely covered.

Next, I checked to see how much damage that rogue spider had done. It was considerably worse than I imagined, I had to core sixty miles of the tube again. That little task was going to set us back another three months. Still, we were so very close to success, all the craters in the chain had been connected. Laser rings already blocked out the Martian environment, all I needed now was to bring that number one tube online and punch the holes.

When I got back to the unit, my day got worse, Zuri was in pain. She wasn't concerned, I was scared stiff.

"Maybe Junior wants to go for another ride," she said calmly.

I told her about the launch pad and that it would be three days before we could lift off, if at all. The pains were sporadic and a few hours apart.

"We have plenty of time," Zuri rubbed the back of my neck. "The baby is probably getting into position, that's all. We have a couple of weeks to go, so don't worry."

She should have told that to the baby, because he had his own schedule. That night, a little after four, a severe pain awakened Zuri. I was sitting in the lounge chair waiting for this moment.

Soft yellow light washed down the walls, barely making her visible. The room was sparsely furnished. There was a small video screen attached to a chair by an adjustable swing tube, a long leathery black couch, which I had made my bed, and a huge air mattress protruding from the wall, with Zuri twisting in the silk bedding.

Six minutes later, she grimaced and let out an earsplitting yell. The blue sheets darkened around her abdomen and we smiled at each other.

I wished we were back aboard Pegasus, but for some reason, all the fear I had was gone. I guess the knowledge that I was only minutes away from becoming a father left little room for any other feelings.

The tri-cart was parked right outside the unit; Zuri eased herself into the seat.

"To the Medical Center, Madame?" I asked lightheartedly.

She grunted through another contraction then reassured me that everything felt fine between them, which were still ten minutes apart.

We came to the airlock of the Medical Center and

it was closed. I peered through the glass. Part of the hallway had collapsed, a red mountain filled the passageway from floor to ceiling. It is possible the structure had been weakened during the fighting and caved in from the weight of the dust. But there was another way into the center; we could exit right here and re-enter through an alternative airlock beyond the blockage, but that meant putting on a soft suit. I didn't want to risk wasting time. Also, I felt the medical center might be contaminated by all the dust.

Another powerful contraction struck and Zuri agreed to go back to our temporary quarters. I propped her up in bed, placed pillows under her knees for comfort, and told her, "I hope you know what to do."

"I must have read every book on the subject by now," she grimaced. "But you are the one with all the brothers and sisters."

"Yeah, the closest I got was Uncle First Class. I did not get involved in this aspect of child care." Although, between my military first aid training and Zuri's instructions, I felt ready. I held a pen laser to cut the umbilical cord in my right hand and Zuri dug her nails into my left.

"God!" she cried out, "those books didn't say it would hurt like this." She was puffing hard and pushing with each contraction.

I saw the crown, its black slick hair sliding in and out of her as she breathed. "OK, I can see him now, you're almost there. Give me a good hard push with the next contraction," I coached. I realized this wasn't going to be as hard as I thought. After all, women had been having babies for thousands of years without computers, neuro-blockers, or even doctors. The head slipped out of sight again and I felt cheated. "C'mon, Honey, you have to push harder."

"Shit! I am. Maybe you'd like to change places," she barked. "This hurt… you… aaurgh!"

Another contraction started and I got ready to cradle the baby's head. Zuri's fists clenched the sheets, and then she screamed so loud I thought she was heard back on Earth. Her body spread slowly and the baby's head popped out up to the neck.

I held the tiny head gently in my left palm. Rivulets of blood mixed with its soft shiny hair and streaked its frowning face. Zuri was breathing heavily, and then another push and the rest of the body flowed into my hands. She sighed and relaxed, then another contraction spewed a pool of dark blood, water, and the placenta out of her.

I cut the baby's cord with the laser, it sealed the end instantly. Then I placed the nose cup over the small ashy face and sucked the fluid from its air passages. "It's a boy," I said softly and held him up for her to see.

He started crying and Zuri cradled him to her breast.

I dropped down on one knee, squeezing her hand between mine, laughing and crying at the same time. "We will name him David," I proclaimed, "the last name in the Bible from the Book of Revelation."

CHAPTER ELEVEN

The sun finally shone on WestPac, three months after David's birth. The dust storms died as suddenly as they began.

David squealed in anticipation, as Zuri took him from the crib.

She cuddled him, saying, "We are going home, my little boy."

The diffused sunrise produced a spectacular rainbow. Mars will always be a desolate and lonely place, I suppose, but I will miss it. The Menninger project is complete, so all that remains, is to blow open the volcanoes. Naturally, we will do that from the safety of our ship.

"Well, Pegasus is still there." I calmed Zuri's fears that somebody might have pirated her. I had just received a full report in the Communication Center. "There were no transmissions recorded by her or observations of any kind. I am beginning to believe that we are the last of the human race."

"What about the far posts and the stations?" Zuri asked with a furrow as she placed David in the pressure pod.

She reminded me of my earlier optimistic views. Opinions that time had eroded. It has been more than a year since the Exchange, and even the few people at Jupiter's fueling facility should be heading earthward.

She said they might have gone straight back, not

bothering to come near Mars at all. And as for those stations around Earth, if they survived, they probably didn't know how or where to contact us. "After all," she reasoned, "only U.S.I. officials would know where the Emergency Procedures sent us."

"Yeah, I guess that's true." I played with David's toes.

The steel canister reminded me of the pet cages people used to transport their cats and dogs. Except this one has a much softer lining and it opens from the top.

Zuri pressed a button on the front of the pod and the lining inflated to cushion David. "Ready?"

"Leave the top open until we are about to lift off, OK?"

"I was," she replied with that warm smile I have seen so much of these days. She pushed the pod along the corridor and I carried two duffel bags of clothes for him. Without the roar of the wind, WestPac has become a crypt once more.

We were taking the X-body back up to Pegasus. The magnetic capsule would have been better but there wasn't room for David's pod. Anyway, without the wind, either ship will fly smoothly. After we have docked, I will retrieve the capsule by remote control.

We dressed in soft suits for the trip. There was no worry in our mind, the pressure pod was secure behind our seats, and David was placidly playing with the air cushion. Not even the rumble of rockets disturbed him. We were on our way home at last.

For the next week or so, I ran system checks on both Pegasus and WestPac's controls. I also conducted at least twenty scans of Mars; I did not want to have another accident. If everything goes well, we will never set foot on Mars again.

That made Zuri very happy.

She spent most of her time with David, but she

managed to give me a hand at nap time. One day she noticed something peculiar, "Did you realize the two probes we sent to Earth stopped transmitting?"

"No, I forgot all about them," I admitted.

"The last signal was in May," she replied, "I came across it while downloading the bridge records."

"It probably doesn't mean anything," I told her. "The probes must have crashed or something."

"What about probe Number Two?" she pressed, "it should still be sending data back."

She had a point, that probe was in orbit outside the dust cloud.

After some thought, I said, "It could have drifted into the cloud too. We will launch a couple more after we get this project up and running smoothly."

The first chance I had I planned to check the probes' data. It didn't seem likely the second probe could drift that far. However, if the cloud expanded or if there was a surge of energy, it could have been caught in it. But right now, the WestPac project was all that concerned me.

Seismic readings were good, the lithosphere was solid. The mantle under the spiders was extremely fluid. Mars had a hard-shell of iron surrounding a lighter larger core. Truly, it is the opposite of Earth's structure. They were ready to plunge the last five-hundred miles under tremendous magnetic pressure. They crushed their way through the brittle rock then controlled the flow around them by expanding to fill the hole.

The lasers within the spiders heated the lava even further. It bubbled through the pipes straight to the surface before being pumped back into Mars' depths. This allowed the lava to rapidly change in density and chemistry.

Steam columns rose to the skies. Thick massive

puffs that spread slowly on the soft Martian winds. The long white clouds snaked across the red sands; the calmness in stark contrast to what we had experienced. This was no longer the Mars we knew or anybody had ever seen.

Clouds grew larger day and night but their massive bodies never shed a drop. Occasionally, dry ice fell on the deserts. Water formed in another manner, deep blue lakes filled our craters. The project was slowly taking shape. Carbon dioxide and ash caused the temperature to rise sharply that summer, and that liberated a lot of the ground water that had been frozen for a million years or more.

Mud slides, or more aptly described, flash floods of blood, ravaged the planet. Deserts turned to seas and rushed into the craters and valleys. The polar caps shrunk, exposing fresh layers of Martian topsoil. But by far though, the greatest changes were in the equatorial region.

Hundreds of miles of rifts suddenly scarred the surface anew. Invisible hands ripped the planet apart before our astonished eyes. Surprisingly, there were no dust storms this time, just the big thick white clouds, rushing bloody rivers, and instant valleys.

The tanks, however, filled slowly. After a month, they were less than a quarter full. I expected this result, but knew that in another month the hydro-pods would start germination.

The project was running so well I didn't have to monitor WestPac at all.

I spent my days with Zuri and David in the habitats. He was walking with the aid of a gravity inhibitor, called a vertical belt. Animals fascinated him. I imagined that since his first three months had been so empty, he was making up for lost time with a passion by chasing anything that moved. And although he never caught any, he never stopped trying. Only Alice curled up with him when he finally tired out.

David wore us out too; keeping up with him was a

full-time job with overtime nightly. He completed our lives. He was smart, intuitive, and with his vertical belt on, he flew after the birds. He followed little foxes down their holes, barking back at the angry mothers in defiance. He was in trouble all the time, and we loved it.

The days passed by so quickly I noticed that we accomplished very little. But I eventually checked the last transmissions from the probes one night while Zuri and David slept.

I was riveted on the data from Number Two, it revealed some startling information. The dust cloud was accreting, particles were not falling back to Earth, as I imagined, but drawing closer together. But the rate of solidification was unsteady. Although I could find no evidence, I was certain the process had crushed probe Number One.

But Number Two... I had a big question mark. There was nothing in the records that remotely suggested it had crashed. And it had never gone closer than a hundred miles of the cloud. It measured a fluctuating gravity field from Earth, but always managed to compensate for it. Therefore, when it simply ceased transmitting, I was left without a clue as to why.

I tried to convince myself Number Two had a system failure, but this too seemed unlikely. The probe housed four independent and identical systems; only complete destruction could silence all of them at once. And I assumed that had occurred, as there were powerful blasts of radiation from Earth periodically. Still, I felt uneasy about Number Two.

I checked Pegasus' sensors for any significant increase in radiation at the time. None was recorded. But a burst of X-rays, such as from a laser, could have destroyed the probe and not been identified by the sensors. A narrow laser beam would be difficult to detect at this distance. As a matter of fact, it is impossible to pick up a laser beam unless one is in line with it. And at the time we were not.

Two burning questions taunted me that night and for days afterwards. If the probe was hit by a laser… who fired it? And why? I decided not to tell Zuri, not yet anyhow. I launched another pair of probes that night. I wanted to get more facts before I informed her of my suspicions.

Christmas was two weeks away; Zack and I were very excited. The whole concept takes on a new meaning when you have a child. David was nine months old and did not have the slightest notion of the celebration, but that did not matter to us. He had plenty of toys to play with already and when Christmas morning arrived, he would have many more.

One of the gifts Zack had Pegasus built, was a holographic player like those in the library. This one was small enough for him to carry. Zack was in the library loading its memory with fairytales when I called.

"Zack, is the baby with you?" I asked.

"No. I thought he was with you, Honey."

His reply numbed my entire body.

"Oh, my God!" Nightmarish visions came to mind. "He was taking a nap and I dozed off… When I woke up just now, he was gone."

"Don't worry," his voice was relaxed, "after all, there is no place he can go. I'll meet you and together we will find him. You remain calm, OK? He probably went chasing after Alice again."

"OK, I'm in our unit."

I was pacing the floor when Zack arrived. Horrible thoughts kept eating at me. Guilt tied my nerves up in tight little knots. Zack gave me a big smile and a hug, and then he brushed my braids from my face.

"Look at you," he said, "the typical overprotective mother. No harm will come to him with the vertical belt on. And it's unlikely he'll fall down a stairwell or something."

I walked over to his crib and held up the black leather belt with its silver discs for him to see. "He must have found a way to unsnap it," I said woefully.

"Oh." The smile disappeared from Zack's face. "He's pretty smart. Look, honey, we will find him. He is probably in one of the habitats."

Before Zack joined me, I had assessed the magnitude of the situation already. We could not use Pegasus' sensors to locate David because we never injected any bionic transponders into him. In fact, we never had him scanned by the Medscan, so Pegasus didn't even have a record of his biorhythm to search for. I suppose Zack knew this also. We started looking in every unit along the way to the habitats.

The fear grew stronger as the minutes turned to hours. We shouted his name over and over, one deck after another, looking in every burrow and den we could find. I knew in my heart that David had encountered some animal and was injured or stuck. "Perhaps he fell down a ladder hole," I panicked.

"Impossible," Zack assured me, "there are covers on all the accesses between the levels. David isn't tall enough to reach the control panels that open them. Anyway, it has been six hours and the little guy ought to be getting hungry. Soon, he will start crying and one of the bots will pick up the sound and relay his position."

"Did you know that David never cries?" My voice was alien to me. I thought about him, I pictured his chubby happy face, those big chestnut eyes, his loud laughter; he was a clone of his father. All these facets of his personality came to me, and I realized David hadn't cried since the day he was born. I shrieked, "Suppose he is on Deck Twenty-two…"

"Pegasus would alert us if that was true."

Zuri was falling apart.

I took her back to our unit and gave her a strong sedative and began to worry about her, and David. I knew if David was dead she would be destroyed.

"God, why are you doing this to us?" I shouted in the empty corridors.

The mini-sub was ready to go by the shore of the lake. This was one search I hoped would fail, one I had to take alone. I crawled into the tight machine from the back and lay on my stomach. It was barely long enough for me to fit into; my face inches from the glass bubble. As I rolled into the water the lights scattered the fish. David was missing for twelve hours now and despair darkened my heart like the murky waters around me.

I navigated around the lake a few feet from the bottom until I reached the drains without any sight of him. I stayed down, looking for his body until my oxygen supply ran out. Back on shore I hoped my luck had been good. I recharged the mini-sub and repeated the search at the beach, with equal results. I should have been relieved, instead, I was sadder. David hadn't shown up at all. Wherever he was, he had to be dying or dead. I do not know how long a baby can survive without food or water, but the fact that no human cries were heard was disheartening.

When Zuri came to I had to confess that David was gone.

I continued the search the next day and the day after that, looking everywhere, pushing my exhausted body to its limits.

Zuri withdrew into catatonia.

I took her to the Medical Center; the sight of her

wired to the machines disgusted me. "What good are they anyway?" I asked myself.

This technology was the best man had ever built. The whole ship was mankind's greatest achievement, yet it could not save my son. Nor could Pegasus stop my wife from dying of a broken heart. Nor did it save humanity. It seemed Pegasus was not the salvation it was purported to be, quite the opposite; it was mankind's damnation. And undoubtedly, the Exchange was someone's cover to hijacking the ship. To what purpose, was still to be determined, but probably not a good one. For anyone.

Zuri's life slowly drained from her body, she grew thin and gray. On Christmas Day, there was nothing except misery as I sat beside her, contemplating our fate.

Things were finally clear to me now, God had not intended for us to survive. We had cheated His all-encompassing wrath and been slowly paying for it ever since. Armageddon had passed and we were stranded and doomed on this devil ship.

One thought throbbed in my mind; and I was sure it was the voice of the Almighty calling us to Him. David was His final sign that death awaited us.

Zuri knew it, and accepted her fate, and all these machines couldn't keep her from it.

I saw it too. And at last, peace will be mine. When Zuri passes through that last door, I am going to overload Pegasus' engines. Blow this damned Dutchman out of God's heaven.

I was on the Bridge preparing; there were many safety features which had to be overridden.

I could not bear to kill Zuri myself, therefore I will wait, however long, or short it takes until she is gone. I transferred the controls to the Medical Center, so I can follow right behind her.

I heated the plasma in the right wing to its limit, then prepared to inject the cold loaded left accelerator with it. The magnetic fields won't be able to contain or control the imbalance. The ship will fizzle away in just a few seconds. No thunderous explosion, no scattering of a million pieces across the heavens. An expanding fiery cloud in the Martian sky will swallow up Pegasus and vanish without a trace.

Inexplicably, I heard singing. Soft and sweet, it was the voice of an angel echoing throughout the ship. 'Twinkle, Twinkle, Little Star', the song Zuri had sung to David every night. Although, it was not Zuri's voice.

At first, I thought I was hallucinating; my mind must have snapped in these final days. Then I figured it was a sign from God, telling me I had made the right decision. That is when the bridge computers went haywire, being reprogrammed at an incredible speed. The monitors flashed messages too fast to read. I was dumbfounded.

The singing stopped and a single message appeared on all the monitors throughout the ship, "Greetings, from Adam One."

I ran to the Medical Center, my heart pounding with fear.

Zuri was sitting zombie-like in her bed. Tears streaming down her face, she said, "It's David! He is alive!"

Too weak to walk, I carried her to the one place we never checked, the Teacher.

And there he sat enthroned like an ancient deity, a multitude of wires making him part of the machine, the soul of Pegasus.

I was relieved and at the same time horrified by the sight.

Zuri cried and sobbed, "My baby, my baby."

For two weeks, he had been tied to the Teacher and

that had an unknown effect on him. Zuri was happy to see her baby alive, I worried that the Teacher had destroyed his mind. We had left the Teacher on maximum output and David had a maximum need to fill. He had wandered into her womb chambers. Or, she had drawn him there like a fly to a spider. She fed him the nourishment he needed, as well as information, downloading material at a voracious rate.

Thirteen days later, David came to the Medical Center, still a baby, but no longer the same.

I had left him with the Teacher and taken Zuri back to recuperate. What use was trying to fight it, whatever had taken place, was irreversible, of that I was sure. And again, I could sense it, monitor and control.

I had been back to see him every day since, and discovered the plethora of changes, but this was the first visit for Zuri.

David stood in the doorway for a while, unnoticed.

I was hunched in my chair, Zuri lay sleeping.

A low giggle ended with a smile.

She sat up and stretched out her arms to him.

"Great Mother, it is pleasing to see you are well." His voice was hardly above a whisper. His features were unchanged but not his expression. Behind that frail voice and careless smile was a cognizance. A great awareness of us, what we felt, what he harbored. "I am sorry I caused you so much pain, Great Mother," he said sincerely, "I did not know before, and I will not again. Is there anything I can do for you?"

"You can hug me. That will make me feel a whole lot better."

CHAPTER TWELVE

Great Mother looked upon me as if nothing had changed, which was true, I was still her baby. She had gone through a great ordeal and her psyche now teetered on the edge of reality, but I knew she would recover as I aged and my mental development reached a more normal level. Because right now, it was far from normal to have a child younger than a year old behave as I was doing. But what disturbed me the most were the thoughts I was getting from Great Father.

He was being torn apart by a sense of guilt for what had transpired, and fear of me. Although he wouldn't admit it, not even to himself, I was no longer his son. I was a monster. My transformation by Pegasus did change my personality, but not in the fashion he imagined.

Then, there was my demon. Pegasus taught me many facts, but knowledge is so much more than an accumulation of facts. I was painfully aware that I lacked life's experiences, and they were needed to help me understand certain concepts, such as God.

Great Father contends that all we do is directed by one force. I have found this to be totally erroneous. What is more, Great Father does not actually believe it either.

One day on the bridge, I was making modifications to the Mars Project when I asked him, "Why were you going to kill yourself by blowing up Pegasus?"

"I was despondent," he replied without hesitation, "the thought of losing you and your mother was too much to bear."

"I understand that," I said, "but why kill Pegasus?"

He looked at me for a long time before answering. His reply, which he knew was wrong, was, "Pegasus is a machine, it has no life."

"You know that is not true," I countered. I was upgrading the Mars Project to include the entire equatorial latitudes. Instead of small pools of life, a garden will encircle the planet. In time, it will cover the entire body. A ground fog, two-feet thick, already persist throughout the region. I designed microbes that aid in the processing of the soil, speeding up the spread of organic substances. I wondered, "Do you consider Mars alive?"

"Mars is a planet," he said in an angry tone. "Planets, rocket ships, space stations are things. There may be living organism on them, in them, but they themselves are not alive."

He remained silent after that, but I still had questions. The most confusing one was, did he understand life? By his reasoning, only organics were alive because they consumed and reproduced.

So does Pegasus. And compared to the microbes, she is a much higher life form.

Again, the question came to mind, "what about God? He neither eats nor reproduces," I pointed out. "Does this make Him a machine?" And then the last one, "Great Father, if our death was so painful, why wait for Great Mother to die? Why delay the suicide?"

He never replied.

I spent most of my time on the bridge and he avoided me by staying in the habitats. Great Mother kept me company and we had lots of fun singing. But there was so much work to do before the arrival of the others that I complained. She just said that was not my responsibility.

"Let your father worry about the project. You should be playing games, and watching cartoons."

I did enjoy them even if they were overly aggressive. But that was part of their appeal, I supposed, being able to survive anything. Cartoons could do the impossible. I needed that escape into the unreal too, and seeing Great Mother's refusal of our world made me sad.

On my birthday, she made a huge cake. It was chocolate with vanilla icing and too big for the three of us. They were happy that day.

While I had this chance to speak to them simultaneously, I explained, "If I was a natural child prodigy, you would be delighted. Therefore, you should realize that I am not different. What the Teacher did for you, it did for me. It made you smarter than you naturally were, it didn't harm you, or change your being. That is what it did for me too; just made me smarter, at a younger age, nothing more." I finally got through to them and was glad.

They appreciated what the Teacher had taught them, even when not aware that she was pushing them beyond their natural capabilities, as without that knowledge they would have been Pegasus' prisoners. And without the Teacher, they believed I would have perished; they were thankful I did not.

About a month later, David was at the communication console. He was sending a message, which was not unusual. We kept several lines open to the probes and WestPac.

As I passed, I was surprised to notice the direction of the beam. "There are no probes in sector seven, David. Who are you radioing?"

"Hermes SX27, Great Father," he replied. "He is lost and can't find Earth. I relayed the correct course so he can complete his mission."

I immediately set the long-range scanners on full power. I could not find a trace of the ship. Curiously, I asked, "How do you know the Hermes is there?"

"I can hear him," he told me honestly, "in my mind."

"You mean by telepathy?" I was amazed.

Not because David had developed this power, because I could feel he had been reading our thought ever since being exposed to the Teacher. What really shocked me was that Hermes SX27 was an automaton.

"Are you telling me that you can read the mind of a computer?"

"It is easier than those of organics," confirmed David. "Theirs has great regularity. Therefore, I can distinguish their wave patterns very easily."

I wondered if he could read the animals onboard Pegasus as well. Instead, I asked, "Why didn't you direct it here?"

"Hermes wants to go home," he stated flatly. "Besides, Earth needs its cargo."

David fulfilled my dreams with that one statement. He was positive that there was organic and mechanical life on Earth. He had learned about different stations' survival while with the Teacher. And then he related their story.

The real war was fought in the black skies above the earth.

Zack saw the cloud formation but still did not believe the amount of destruction that took place in such a short time. All out nuclear war or the MAD (Mutual Assured Destruction) principle had been discussed and debated after the bombing of Hiroshima and Nagasaki. With little more than computer models and theories to go on, no one could accurately predict the outcome or the amount of devastation such an event would generate.

The Star Wars Defense System, a network of Earth and Space based pulse-laser cannons known as SWDS, was touted to be ninety-five to ninety-nine percent effective against MAD. David surmised it operated at ninety-nine percent efficiency for the first few minutes.

But the initial blasts did more than destroy a dozen major cities; it created holes in the network by blinding some of the targeting satellites, allowing the projectiles to strike other targets. And not all the ballistic missiles that were hit by laser pulses were completely neutralized. New generation ballistic missiles were built to let the rocket bodies explode and jettison their warheads intact.

Each subsequent impact further weakened the fragile crust, making the next strike increasingly more devastating. The nuclear blasts super-heated the atmosphere decreasing the overall pressure so more material was thrown farther into space at higher speeds.

Then, there was the effect of the RGPs. The enormously energetic projectiles caused even greater ejections to be launched into the heavens. It was as if the Earth was undergoing a meteor bombardment of prehistoric proportions during a nuclear war. Over and over, mountainous quantities of rock were ejected.

Since strikes did not have to be precise to be effective, all land and sea based SWDSs were gone within the first two minutes. After that, only space-based laser cannons were left to protect the world, and that was never a viable option. As the bombardment intensified, Earth erupted, spewing tons of molten rock into space. The matter froze in the icy vacuum creating the black cloud observed by Zack.

The debris was then trapped by the artificial gravity of Colonies and Space Station that surrounded the planet. The force fields designed to protect the space communities instead created the deadly cloud that was the outcome of the MAD doctrine.

Major cities were hit hard at the outset and seventy-five percent of the population died in the first minutes. The remaining conflicts were between military fortifications, and without a populace to protect, they fought to ensure their own survival.

The nuclear devastation of cities—most reduced to white hot rubble—was dwarfed by the igneous laser beams. It became a war of wait and fire. They charred earthbound bases and space stations alike as they came into range. Identification was impossible under the heavy blanket of radiation and the battle quickly boiled down to the last gunfighter standing winning it all.

Space stations survived the longest, earth bases crumbled due to the aftershocks of nukes and RGPs. But the number of stations dropped fast as they were picked off within the murky cloud. At the start of the Exchange, some linked to each other, like the branches of a hydra. The backbone of these space creatures were the laser satellites, and the one determined to be the last gunfighter was U.S.S.D.S.

General Newton acted swiftly, as his years of training had conditioned him to, and with shrew reasoning. Under his umbrella, he gathered eighty percent of the diplomatic corps. Twelve of the major stations joined the network without delay, accepting his position as acting governor for the duration, the U.S.I. colonies being among the first. Colony 5 was towed and joined to U.S.I.'s medical facility, Colony 3. Those who did not join were fired upon through the darkness. The precise disabling of stations' life support systems and power relays forced quick surrender, or lingering death.

The general understood the hardships of war, as well as the agony of survival, so he promptly terminated all sentences in the penal colonies.

Lieutenant Charles faithfully transmitted the signal that seared the nerves of thousands of prisoners.

Transponders, barely the thickness of a baby's hair, electrocuted them in a matter of seconds. It was very efficient and very military. Lieutenant Charles leapt from his seat, "May I be excused, Sir?"

"Remain at your station, Lieutenant. We are not done here, not even close to victory. And trust me, I know how you feel. But those lives were not wasted; their quarters will be modified and reassigned. Their bodies decomposed for fertilizers, something we are in short supply of," reported the General.

The latter was the actual reason behind the executions, to feed livestock and make room for them to multiply. Eight penal colonies were converted to farms, one remained a prison.

While ambassadors hastily formed a new group to replace U.N.A.S.C., the General tightened the net. He ordered full scale reconstruction of the stations; a move that endeared him to the bewildered, and made him politically stable. By centralizing the work, he manipulated who got workers, supplies, and the type of repairs performed.

Within a few days, mankind gave rise to yet another great ruler of the world. Or, it should rather be said, Gen. Christopher Newton appointed himself, and a relic of due process approved his ascension to the throne.

Robots remodeled the prisons for pigs, cows, and fowl, they prepared the feed, and fertilized the new fields. The new era in human history began operating as smoothly as a jump-jet. Except for the prisoners, life rolled on like the eternal night.

I formed a few theories of how David knew these facts, though, I never asked for verification. I listened and accepted his words as Gospel, because he had probably read the log entries of U.S.S.D.S., or maybe General Newton's mind, or, everyone's.

"Then, our next move," I announced, "is back to Earth!"

The stations were interlocked by steel tubes. All habitation stations required light energy to function and were fed by lasers from the defense station.

General Newton claimed he needed the nuclear power from the other stations to support the entire system and used fear tactics to convince those in the habitats that it was safer within the cloud.

"Once outside the cover of clouds, you will be vulnerable to attack from rogue sats set to destroy anything they encounter. We have no way of knowing how many, or where these satellites are. There may be other stations or ships operating outside the cloud, pirates if you will, waiting to ransack or take over your facilities. The only way to ensure everyone's safety is to stay together and we will all leave when the time is right."

Honobi Hamabutu, a senior member of U.N.A.S.C., led a powerful coalition that was on the verge of centralizing all the stations. He was strongly backed by Gen. Christopher Newton because he agreed it was best to wait until it was safe. Hamabutu was the highest official of the U.S. of Africa and controlled half of the surviving agri-businesses. The other half, along with eighty percent of the manufacturing trade, was owned by U.S.I. But they were tired of waiting for the invisible enemy to emerge.

Captain Brolocci, a full board member, disagreed heatedly with the general. "We have more than enough ships to protect our station and anyone else who wants to join us. We need to return to a higher orbit and assess the situation. Repairs are progressing at a snail's pace because of the risk of contamination. We cannot afford to wait for your ghosts to become reality."

Truth was, the captain knew Pegasus was waiting for them, and it had more than enough resources for the surviving human race. Newton never asked about it and Brolocci thought it wiser not to mention it either. He was not sure if the general had made any attempts to capture the ship, and therefore did not want to give her position away. U.S.I. had plans to let others onboard, but it was on their own terms.

The general kept them all in check though, with periodic phantom raids, highly visible patrols, and most effective, mandatory forty-eight-hour duty time every week. That made certain any independent efforts crawled towards completion. Those who opposed him, accidently lost personnel while on duty. Newton constructed a black web out of the ashes of Hell and snared one eight thousand flies, to devour at leisure.

Brolocci came up through the military, and he knew when to acquiesce to the General's will. He believed the war hadn't ended yet; there was still the General himself to battle. But they had to prepare, be ready to escape before that battle began.

He did his forty-eight with great care, since flying patrols were the riskiest duty, there was danger of contamination from the radioactive dust they flew through. A rocket with a faulty seal was certain to return a dead pilot. Also, the instruments were nearly useless because of the radiation, many of the pilots smashed into large unseen debris in the hazy cloud.

Their flight path always kept them in the mire. The general insisted that restrictive flight paths were necessary to ensure security and prevent pilots from getting hopelessly lost. Any course deviation got them blasted by an unseen incoming projectile. Defense stations had railguns, which fired smaller darts but just as deadly as their larger counterparts. These were the original designs of the twentieth century, made to destroy ships and rockets.

The stations' force fields held the dust a mere five hundred meters from the network, and a pilot had to know when and where his window would appear. There was little room for error or time for corrections. If a ship came out of the clouds on a collision course, it was summarily blown away.

General Newton would say, "It is better to lose one man, or one ship, then half a station and thousands of lives."

Of course, anyone who went beyond the cloud could never reorient himself; and to return was as fatal as to continue into deep space.

Captain Brolocci thought about Pegasus a great deal, and that she was waiting for them, but the short range of the patrol rocket-ship could never reach her. Their only way of escape was to contact her. But the cloud kept them from her. That is, the cloud, and General Newton.

The general was trained to make his will law and reluctant to surrender this power. He was a man addicted, a very long time now, to a very powerful drug, and the very thought of losing that drug was more terrifying than death. It caused him to do anything to maintain his supply. For the general, murder, either one at a time, or in masses, kept his supply of power steady.

The governor of Juno, the Italian wheel, had secret plans to break from the network and when Newton learned of his treason, he shorted out their protective field. The deadly smoke infiltrated the city before anyone could seal the vents. The entire population was exposed to high levels of radiation.

Arlene was working on Juno at the time. Her hair fell out five minutes after the treachery, and the burning in her lungs was soothed only by her own blood. She coughed thick red fluid from her mouth for an hour and then she lay down stone dead. It was the same throughout the giant wheel. And would have been the same throughout the entire network if not for the airlocks between stations. They automatically closed at the loss of the protective field.

After the fifteen thousand died in the Juno accident, the General's power was solidified. There were only three monthly meetings of the Action Planning Board after the accident. No one raised the possibility of breaking up the network again.

David could talk no longer; the long day had exhausted him. A brilliant red glow, like Mars ablaze, shone on his face. It was a statue's face, no emotion, no grief, not a sign that the story had affected him whatsoever.

I can't say I was shocked either, just saddened that mankind had spawned yet another tyrant.

David positioned eighteen probes of various types around the Earth, some on the planet, others in the dust cloud, all relaying information twenty-four hours a day, and learned things he could not comprehend. The Earth had yet to die, this he knew. So why did they wait to leave it?

CHAPTER THIRTEEN

Bob Marshall was suiting up for his patrol. He was doing a tight round, flying the outside hundred with Brolocci. This flight was going to be extremely dangerous, as both were part of the U.S.I.'s breakout team.

The outside hundred was the area beyond the cluster of stations at one hundred miles—thousands of miles from the outer edge of the cloud—but supposedly clear of any derelict stations. The space beyond that was reportedly littered with fragmented stations and satellites, large and small. The outside hundred had been cleared by a constant barrage of laser fire. That was, as far as their sensors could penetrate the cloud.

Ever since Arlene's death, they had begun working on a clandestine plan to abandon the stations, and started building new spiders to quickly fashion solar power shields and habitats. The U.S.I. executives counted on the General taking their colonies in exchange for their freedom, but in case he did not, they wanted to be ready. They planned to warn him to clear their flight path at launch time. If he did not, U.S.I. was prepared to fire RGPs at the laser cannons, leaving the station defenseless but intact.

Bob was about to execute the second step in the plan. He was going to extend his flight to the edge of the cloud. From there, he would fire a small satellite with a metallic optic line. This would be their eyes and ears so they could aim their launch tubes.

As they approached their apogee, Bob peered deep

into the blackness, and wondered if it was day or night. His ship's chronometer said six hundred hours, but nobody relied on them anymore. There was no way to confirm their accuracy since they could not determine how fast the dust was traveling.

Furthermore, the General had them drifting around for a few months after the Exchange. Time of day is relative to the sun's position and sunlight did not penetrate this cloud. Bob could see faint rainbows at times as the light reflected off ice particles. Sailing with Captain Ahab, he wasn't sure if it was dawn's light or dusk's, or somebody who could not fly straight.

Bob reached the breakpoint and opened the throttle all the way; he had to complete the mission and rejoin Brolocci before he crossed the field. They were only a hundred miles deep and he had no idea how thick the ooze was. A thousand miles and nothing… He had only two and a half minutes before he had to launch the satellite.

He wanted to go back and say, "I set it out in the sunshine." But that was not to be. As time ran out, he fired it into the inky residue, a cord running behind the tiny communicator.

Bob tried to push the rocket faster than its top speed could handle, because people on the defense satellite took the word 'deadline' seriously. A minute and a half had gone by and Brolocci's tail lasers were not visible. Had he strayed? Two minutes… yes, there went the green flasher and just to its left was the red one.

A few minutes later, he released the optic line's anchor. It would align itself with Colony 5's tower. They would receive the data by remote optical codes.

'They will also send a code,' Brolocci thought. Not that they would wait for Pegasus, but hopefully, they would rendezvous with it in space. The colony launch facilities had been widened since the bombing, now, they could start work on the drivers. This was the final phase of their

escape plan.

Bob's biceps tightened as he fired the retro-rockets at full throttle. Seconds before he hit the barrier, the ship did a nine G roll, turn and flip. He was knocked out by the force.

Captain Brolocci fired a magnetic lock and line on Bob's ship. "Control, this is Patrol One. Bob Marshall is down . . . repeat, Patrol Two is down and…"

"Patrol One, give clearance and we will take it out," Lieutenant Charles said sullenly.

"Negative, Lieutenant! I have him under tow and I'm bringing him in," the captain raged.

"Now, hear this, Captain!" Newton flared from some dark corner of his web. "That ship is a danger to every person in this network. I won't have it crashing, contaminating and fouling my decks. Stand clear or both ships will be destroyed. Now!"

The captain was unimpressed. He slowly and calmly radioed back, "He's my man, and my ship, and we will land at Colony 5. Out."

Bob had come to, "Thanks. I'd like to fry his ass one day."

"Forget it; we are landing in Bay B7 in a minute."

The two ships streaked past the long black windows of the tubular Colony 3. Behind them, laser turrets flashed beams of energy to solar dishes. The sharp corners of the defense station stood out in the center of smooth curves. The square peg in a round hole had a perfect sightline throughout the network. There was always a laser turret looking over their shoulders.

Lieutenant Charles sat at his console and thankfully watched the tiny ships fly home.

David suggested a trip to WestPac would be good for us.

Mars was transformed considerably since he took over the project. He has low altitude bio-sats working the planet's atmosphere. They contain enzymes that synthesize methane, carbon dioxide, water, and other useful gases. The ultraviolet light, which is very strong, powers the reactions, and the satellites remain in a fixed position by magnetic beams.

We could walk around in soft suits because of the increased atmospheric pressure. The air, however, was a deadly mixture. It was a pale blue warm haze that rose from a cotton-like frost at our knees. The ground was spongy with bristles. The sun had turned into a hard and sharp ball, its light no longer diffused by the dust. The planet appeared fresh, a virgin world ready for life. High in the skies, great silky veils floated. And at dusk, a brief sprinkling of rain crossed the rocky desert plains. It wouldn't be long before they vanished under the creeping tundra.

David reversed the course of nature in just eight months. In a few years, Mars will be a living planet.

"Then the others will have a home," he remarked.

Curiously, I asked him, "Do you think our crew will make it?"

"You refer to the crew of Colony 5, but I mean Pegasus' crew. They are the ones we prepare for." He looked at me with sadness, "The people of Earth are on the verge of extinction. They must leave the dust cloud in a matter of days if they plan to survive. All indications reveal they are on an indefinite time scale."

"How can the end be so close and they not know it?" I was unconvinced.

David had to be wrong; Pegasus was feeding him bad data or something. I saw the same facts and figures and did not draw that conclusion.

"You have to take the cloud as part of the entire system. A while ago I told you earth had not finished its alterations. But the dramatic convergence of the nuclear cores within will start the finale," David informed the both of us. "The end will be very quick; the cores will blast an enormous amount of Earth's liquid mantel spaceward. Stirred by the bombardment, the cloud will accrete at a rapid rate. Those who do not evacuate before then, will become part of a new moon. Now, I believe it is time for you to meet your crew."

We climbed into the cockpit of the sleek jump-jet.

I fired up the three aft turbine engines and they greedily sucked in the new air. We roared above the deserts of Mars, heading for the great secret of Pegasus. I could not conceive of the difficulties I was facing.

Newton called the young lieutenant to his office.

Once, lieutenant Charles had been eager to be part of the general's team. But that faded along with his youthful outlook. He learned to distrust and fear his superiors, especially the general. This world dulled his boyish shine and a gray shadow stained his cheek. Blackness shaded his eyes just as duty darkened his soul. He received bizarre orders at an escalating pace.

This time, the general sent a detachment to Colony 5.

"I know you are close to some of the people there," Newton culled. "I want you to head the security unit. Get a feel for what's going on. You know what I mean?" He sat in front of a neon map of the network, his hair and skin ghastly green in the dimly lit office.

Here was a man demented by the almightiness of his office. Now, he needed spies.

The lieutenant left the office feeling relieved. He had made sure all information out of the U.S.I. colonies came through him. He did have contacts in the colonies; Bob Marshall was one of his best friends, who was wise, rough, and brutally honest. A man he totally trusted. They were happy to bring him up to date on their escape plans and he gladly fed them the information they lacked.

The plan was auspicious indeed, they moved people into their hospital and prepared to evacuate from there. Three freighters sat on tracks awaiting the magnetic pulsators that would hurtle them to freedom. They carried the spiders, their hopes, and a good deal of their luck. Ships that would carry the population—most in hibernation—waited on the lower levels. There were some on board already, on racks like slabs of meat.

Only about five percent of people would be awake to run the ships, as a skeleton crew was all they could afford to feed. Until the spiders built the first agriculture station, the populace would have to be kept inanimate.

The satellite Bob launched faced earth, and the lieutenant gave them the final data they needed to aim their launch tubes. He supplied statistical data on their orientation, so they could plot rendezvous points before liftoff. When the exodus began, spiders would set on a direct course to the asteroid belt. The rest would await their return in a sector beyond the moon. The exact location was kept a secret; the course was already in the guidance computers. When the time came, Lieutenant Charles would order his men to secure the launch tower.

Their wish was to evacuate everybody who could get to Colony 5 in time.

The lieutenant would make sure certain airlocks remained open. In the end, Bob, Brolocci, and himself would be launched into space aboard the tower. Exhaust from the nuclear generators, would drive them and all who reached its flight decks.

David led us deep into Pegasus, through corridors I had never visited.

He stopped the tri-cart on Deck Forty-four and said,

"Prepare to meet your crew."

The tri-cart jerked forward and bright yellow light shone from portals on either side.

We rolled slowly through the spotlights, there was a hazy fluid behind the glass bubbles. Halfway through, he stopped again, hundreds of spotlights crisscrossed the corridor.

He approached one of the portals. The light wiped out his features. He gave us a gentle wave and we knelt beside him. Behind the glass was a fetal form. David held out his hand, and the baby did the same.

I looked in another portal and found another fetus in a different stage of development. Throughout the maze of corridors from floor to ceiling and all through Deck Forty-four each incubator nurtured a child.

David left us there, saying simply, "Now you know the full scope of Pegasus."

Still in awe, we rejoined David on the bridge hours later. But before we could start the barrage of questions, he announced that our orbital alignment had been changed. Instead of pointing head down at WestPac, we were belly-out and picking up speed. We were leaving orbit, but not by David's command.

"When I returned to the bridge," he told us, "the computers had received orders to return to Earth."

"Who's orders?" I asked bitterly.

"They were unidentified," he said calmly, "they were on the same code level that started the incubation. However, whoever has summoned us, will not be alive to meet the ship. By my calculations, they have about twelve hours left and they programmed the ship to take a three-month course."

"Then we have to help them," I ordered. "They are expecting us to rescue them; we've got to do something,

David!”

"We can try to warn them of the eminent danger,” he said reluctantly.

"What if they don't get the message? What else can we do?”

"Great Father, I know what you're thinking,” David answered crossly. "There is a million to one chance of altering their fate by physical intervention. Maybe a billion to one.”

"We have to try,” I implored.

David did not share my reasoning; to him, their death would come as a quick surprise. He saw no sense in risking the ship or its inhabitants. "These are the very people who caused this dilemma. They are receiving their own tragic justice.”

"What about those who did not contribute to the destruction of the Earth? Do they deserve to die too?” I challenged him.

He looked at me with disgust. "That is precisely why they built Pegasus, so their children would live and grow, continue human culture and further their dreams of peace.”

He almost had me convinced it was best to do nothing. After all, that is what I have been doing, nothing. I told myself for three years that I was saving the ship. I had myself believing I was somehow helping mankind by staying on Mars. But if I had really meant to help them, I would have turned Pegasus around as soon as I took over control. Now that the final hours were at hand, there was nothing I could do, merely feeling safe in letting Pegasus control our destiny. Or, as I knew I had to, take action. I had to persuade David to take the risk; he was the only hope we had of beating the odds.

"David, remember when you asked me why I hesitated destroying Pegasus if your mother's impending death hurt me so bad?” I began explaining.

We sat eye to eye, Zuri had a hand on each of our shoulders.

"I didn't know the answer then, and it took a long time before I figured it out myself. It was the same force that has driven us since the Exchange. The same rationale they used when Pegasus, and its life forms, were sent to Mars. The same power that has driven humans from the start. It is hope. It is the last belief to die. After we lose our faith in Justice, then God's mercy, we still hold onto the hope we will survive. That is why I could not kill Zuri. I could not destroy this ship until there was no hope at all. That is why Pegasus was sent to Mars, and not directly to New Eden. And this proves it unequivocally. Back on Earth, someone is hanging on by a thread. That thread is hope."

"This I do understand," he said flatly.

But I failed to sway his judgment.

"When you planned to blow up this ship, Pegasus stopped you. She interrupted my teachings and ordered me to call out to you. Then she transferred command to me when she knew you were unfit to continue doing so. She will not allow us to destroy her, not by any means. Great Father, you once gave a bot orders to crash her if you did not return. But Pegasus would never have permitted those orders to be executed. Do you understand," David begged, "it is not that I do not wish to help them, Pegasus will not perform any task that endangers its existence."

Finally, Zuri spoke, her voice a whisper, "Pegasus is only a machine. The people who built her tried to foresee every possible event, planned for every conceivable reality, and of course, fell short of the mark. They had to, nobody can see the future. They may have had an inkling this situation might arise, but I am sure they felt somebody would alter their plans. David, you are the only person who can make the changes. You are the hope they are holding onto. You must reprogram Pegasus!"

She did not move him either. David sat stone-faced throughout our pleas.

Pegasus had taught him that she was the only hope of mankind. He knew that to save one person, on one station, he would jeopardize all life. To David, or Pegasus, I was not sure which, our arguments were insane.

In desperation, I asked him, "What will you tell Pegasus' children?"

"I don't have to tell them anything," he responded, "Pegasus is teaching them everything, just as she taught me."

"Everything, except how to be human," I said coldly. "The only thing that separates us from other creatures, or machines in this circumstance, is that we are willing to sacrifice our lives to benefit others. That is why we hold onto that last breath, that is why we have hope. If we allow those people to die without trying to help, we will never be able to implant the only seed that saves mankind; the ability to care, to love, and revere life itself."

Great Father clarified a lot of concepts I did not comprehend. Then, they left me alone on the bridge to re-program Pegasus computers. I did not agree with everything either said, but I did grasp they had more to lose than Pegasus, to whom I explained there was only one chance to save the people in the cloud.

What I did know was that to attempt this we had to arrive at the precise moment the shockwave from Earth hit them. Traveling at the speed of light, we would have to use our momentum via magnetic beams to break up the cloud and allow them to escape. My main problem was convincing Pegasus that flying into an unstable gravita-tional system would not cause her to crash, which it proba-bly would.

The General read the latest report from his lieutenant; it told him the epidemic was spreading fast.

Eighty percent of U.S.I.'s personnel were confined to the infirmary. Other stations had reported being infected as well. He did not believe the reports for a second; what he did believe was that his spy had become a turncoat.

Newton felt his hold on the network slipping. But this time, he would put down the rebellion with concrete actions. *'A laser blast to U.S.I.'s corporate headquarters should bring everybody back in line.'*

The General's brooding was interrupted by his chief science officer, Brad Wolf. His report was much more alarming than that of Lieutenant Charles.

He told Newton of the impending doom. "Sensors confirmed this morning the hot spots we have been tracking are speeding up. They are now swirling pools of lava, the smallest is the size of Wisconsin, that's over sixty-five thousand square miles." Wolf handed over a stack of papers with graphs and pictures. Then he continued in an agitated state. "All the smaller nuclear sites have combined into these three super cells. They are at least a mile deep and continuing to grow. They are also converging. In less than a day the cells will merge."

"And how is this my problem?"

"It will be," said Brad Wolf sternly. "It will be everyone's problem when those cores collide. The Convergence will be cataclysmic. Their density will be so great they will drop to the center of the earth. Rapidly. And in this case, what goes down must come up. Understand?"

"How big of an explosion are we looking at?"

"Conservative estimates say the ejected mass could be five times as much as what's in orbit already. Anything and everything in its path will be destroyed. We must get out of orbit immediately."

The general smiled at Wolf's departing frame.

Within minutes, he ordered all his people back to their posts then had them reinforce the airlocks between the battle-station and the eight converted prisons. He knew they needed to break from the cloud before the convergence of nuclear masses and the eruption it would cause, but the station's laser cannon would effortlessly clear a path to deep space. He planned to wait until the last minute before pulling the twenty-five-thousand-man station out of the network, deliberately stranding the rest of the stations, especially U.S.I., and Lieutenant Charles, the turncoat. Let them face the bombardment to come.

Chilton and Marshall were securing the injured aboard the hospital ship, Freedom Seven. They could not be placed in hibernation because the process had ill-effects on recuperation. Instead, they attached an auxiliary power unit to Edwin Puma's bed, who had suffered head injuries during the sabotage, and was comatose.

Chilton, assigned as captain of the ship, was on full alert and prepared to launch at a moment's notice. The U.S.I.'s science team was still debating the best possible launch time. The probe Marshall had fired out of the cloud had put U.S.I. on high alert. They were preparing for immediate evacuation.

While some felt that they should leave before the catastrophic convergence of the cores, others argued that the ships lacked sufficient amounts of slag in their hulls. Slag was a good insulation against the tremendous amount of radiation that would be released and the ships had to rely on their magnetic fields if they were in space when the waves hit. Many believed they could ride out the initial shockwave in the station, which had a thick layer of slag for protection. Others feared more than just the radiation. Although, all agreed that radiation would hit first.

Lieutenant Charles waited for Captain Brolocci's orders to cut power to the laser turrets covering the launch tower. The minutes were filled with tension; he had heard the recall orders, everyone knew the General was plotting something.

The lieutenant had reported his men afflicted by the mysterious virus a week ago, thus exempting them from the recall. All secondary access to Colony 5 had been sealed and the main corridor was under armed guard. With each tick of the clock and every heartbeat, his patience waned. But he was a good soldier; he would wait for his orders to bring down the station's weapon computers. He prayed the general had not revoked his clearance.

David called us back to the bridge; he had calculated when the convergence would occur.

"We will increase to light speed in ten minutes," he informed us, "if anything goes wrong, I want us to be together." He sat in the captain's chair, his body dwarfed by its size.

I saw fear in his eyes and noticed his body trembling.

"The cloud is very dense now; it has become a fat oval with two thin branches encircling the Earth. Our focal point will be the back end of the oval, so we can drive the stations spaceward."

I leaned over and kissed him gently on the forehead. Brushing down his curly black hair, I said, "I love you, David."

"I love you too, Great Mother," he whispered. "Let me tell you the three possibilities we face. One, if we arrive too soon or too slow we will be drawn into the cloud and suffer the same fate as the others. Two, if we arrive too late or traveling faster than light speed the stations shall be crushed and we will impact like an egg against a stone wall. And finally, if everything does go right, there is still the possibility that Pegasus will bounce off the shock wave into the sun.

"Into the sun!" Zack cried.

"Because we need to use the gravitational drivers of the ship, that... is a definite possibility," David confirmed. "The sun will be the strongest attraction. It's not too late to cancel the plan, Great Father."

"Yes, it is," I assured him. I had no intention of spending my life second guessing.

He told us to strap in and that once we went to light speed, he would take over control from Pegasus' computers.

At first, the cloud was just a speck, but it grew quickly as we approached, and the sun a horrid blue-green due to our speed. There was no sense counting down the minutes, it would all be over soon enough. Suddenly, there was a sensational burst of blinding light.

Edwin Puma abruptly tore his restraints from his bed screaming, "Pegasus! Pegasus! Pegasus!"

Captain Brolocci started the launch sequence, and the huge laser guns fired into the muddy dust, burning three immense holes in the cloud. "Launch the spider ships," he ordered.

Great columns of flames leaped from the newly formed outlets.

General Christopher Newton yelled to his crew, "The time is here, all drivers, full power!"

Throughout the network, the uninformed populace scurried in blind panic.

Shockwaves ripped through the black mass, the energy of lasers and rockets turning the gas blazing red. Huge chunks, boulders, careened in every direction, some bounding off the stations massive energy fields. Some crashed through them, the agricultural stations taking the most damage, as they were made of thin crystalized metals, too fragile for the amounts of energy and matter thrown against them.

Pegasus bucked and kicked, then, she lunged towards the sun. I knew I could not stop her; our only chance was to focus on one of the larger sunspots. As the sun's surface cools, it creates the dark areas, which grow heavy and sink back into the sun's interior. I locked Pegasus' magnetic beams on one and allowed it to pull us in.

Our speed was many times that of light and the sunspot, which stretched hundreds of thousands of miles in every direction, acted as a shield against the unimaginable solar bombardment. I could not tell how deep we penetrated the sun, or if it blew us out of the way.

I felt the energy of thousands struggling to survive. From a single blade of grass to every child onboard, Pegasus sucked in energy. Her photosphere swelled and expanded to counteract the power of the sun. It was the will to live as much as her nuclear power that would determine the ship's fate. It was over in a millisecond. Pegasus was ejected in an enormous solar flare.

She tumbled through space encased in deuterium, suffering heavy damages to its outer shell.

We will not be able to repair her until our deuterium cocoon disintegrates. In fact, we will not know where we are or where we are headed until that time. We do know that we are alive, and that was my objective.

THE END

EPILOGUE

Brolocci lead the argosy as far as Mars, where they found an unexpected home awaited them. He had anticipated seeing Pegasus, but after viewing the colony's records knew that although she was absent now, she had been here, and provided for their arrival. There was no record of Pegasus receiving her recall orders either, but Brolocci noted that she had left orbit at that time.

David had not recorded his plan to save the people of Earth.

As he told his parents, "If we fail and are destroyed, but somehow manage to save even a small portion of people and colonies there, they would search for us in vain. They need to move forward with their lives, so it is the humane thing to do. If all goes well, we will contact them."

They were also aware that if they succeeded, colonists would need supplies of nearly everything they lost on Earth. Pegasus had the units meant for Alpha Centauri…

Zack said, "These units won't be usable here for a couple of decades, but if our friends do make it this far then perhaps they can take them to Alpha Centauri. It is a fraction of what was lost, but it will mean a lot."

"And if Alpha Centauri is no longer the objective, they can create a new start here, or, in time, back on Earth," concluded Zuri.

Zack and Zuri off-loaded agricultural and livestock units that were kept in stasis until the planet would be ready for habitation. It was to be a respite on their journey to Alpha Centauri.

Brolocci searched for Pegasus for a few years but came up empty, then, sent signals ahead to Alpha Centauri, in hopes she had gone to complete her mission. He did not expect an answer right away, but if Pegasus reached the system and dropped out of hyperspace, he was hoping for restored communications.

Three, four, five years passed and no message. His conclusion, Pegasus had returned to Earth as commanded and was destroyed in the violent aftermath of the Convergence. He abandoned hope.

The Earth was a hot molten ball of rock blanketed in a steamy cloud. Returning to Earth would be impossible for decades, if not longer. Small meteors pelted her daily as the debris from mankind's foolishness rained. Nothing had survived, nor would live there again. Earth returned to her primordial state.

They built a new Pegasus, a simplified model of the original. The spaceport was brought to Mars where construction took place. They didn't need many of the habitats since they had few livestock. They hoped Alpha Centauri could provide the variety of life they desperately missed. A few stayed behind, content to make Mars—a familiar place, their new home.

Everything happened so fast, Zack and Zuri were unaware if David had been successful.

In the split second while they were near Earth, David saw several ships escaping the cloud. The shockwave produced by Pegasus was like a cue ball hitting the racked balls on a pool table, the stations on the outside ejected from the pack. It was a chaotic event, with some of the stations exploding, or being torn apart by the enormous energies surging through the cloud. Hundreds of thousands lost their lives, especially on the agricultural stations, which were not built to withstand such forces. Their glass exteriors shattered, casting its inhabitants into the roiling mass. While the main body of the stations, U.S.S.D.S., absorbed the force and remained in place.

The cloud also clumped together in spots and created massive rock formations, probably from the magnetic force fields of the stations, concluded David. He told his parents that there had been a great power drain on Pegasus' atomic accelerators. A huge bow wave of energy from the Earth joined with Pegasus' and preceded her to the Sun. This immense energy, along with the collective desire to live fed Pegasus' aurora. It enabled her to withstand the radiation.

The ship bounced off the surface of the sun, its aurora acting as an outer skin. It was much like skipping a stone off a lake, however, the charged particles of the sun's chromosphere had been pulled away and enveloped them.

David related Edwin Puma's story about Earth being populated by the spirits of the Sun. He rejoiced in knowing they were the children of that legend. It spoke of an everlasting peace.

Years would pass before Pegasus emerged from the darkness of the sun. She orbited the solar system as a dead asteroid, no life or energy shining through her cocoon. Pegasus released a multitude of tiny spiders, not to eat through the dense thick layer, but to score lines along its shell. It used the deuterium as fuel for the atomic accelerators. Whispery lines ran down from the spiders back to their mother, feeding her.

When the proper number of stress fractures and fissures were carved, we fired up the accelerators and cracked the shell open.

It was another decade before the ship reached the planet with two moons, one very old and the other brand new. Pegasus landed softly on the crisp black Earth. The air was fresh and smelled sweet like after a summer rain. But it was quiet, no bird songs in the pale blue sky, no insects clicking across the vast barren land.

In the years before their arrival, rain had fallen continuously. Even in the winter months, rain mixed with snow drenched the arid land. Fresh lakes and oceans filled in the low lands, their waters undisturbed by any living creature. One gigantic continent stretched across the equatorial region virtually dividing the planet in halves. Three rivers raced from the north to the south a thousand miles wide and another ten times vaster flowed slowly in the other direction.

Now Zack, Zuri, David, and the five thousand children of Pegasus were the first organisms to inhabit the planet again, although, they were children no longer. Pegasus had kept the five thousand in the incubators until they reached six years of age, then let them assume the duties each was trained for.

Incubators were deactivated, Pegasus had a full complement of personnel.

Zack felt them probing his mind, but what they searched for, he could not tell. He did find it strange that there was no second generation born aboard Pegasus, because as far as he could see, there was something missing in their lives.

Appropriately, they called their home, New Eden. And gradually, they would turn this barren land into a fertile world once more.

The new moon, partially buried in a dark turbulent towering cloud, was the only remnant of the past. Lightning arched within and fierce bolts rocketed Earthward from time to time. More often, the discharges were spiked upward, striking the surface of the moon they called Deminus. Although it looked ominous, they considered it to be of little importance. Pegasus' analysis concluded the discharges would wane and eventually cease, as the cloud coalesced into the moon, or the heavier particles fell back to Earth.

Locked deep within that crypt was the power that had caused this transformation.

General Christopher Newton had failed to escape as tons of molten rock were compressed around him by the combined forces of the Convergence and Pegasus' timely arrival. His own insane attempt to hold onto power caused the debris to be drawn around him. Over the years, he charged his people to dig their way out. It was an improbable task, directed by an irrational man-made god.

His was a dark world, inhabited by people without hope or desire, but three of the prisons had survived. They produced a dwindling supply of meat for the inhabitants of Newton's Kingdom. The livestock could not reproduce fast enough to keep up with demand, and without agricultural units, they were slowly starving. Sacrifices had to be made.

Their life was a joyless daily ritual that ended in despair. Death was the only hope of relief and many gladly welcomed it.

About The Author

A native New Yorker, born and raised in the Bronx, James L Hill spent his adolescence years in Fort Apache, the South Bronx 41st precinct during the 60's, during a time when you needed to have a gang to go to the store. Raised on blues, soul, and rock and roll gave him the heart of a flower child. Educated by the turmoil of Vietnam, Civil Rights, and the Sexual Revolution produced a gladiator. Realizing the precariousness of life gave him an adventurous outlook and willingness to try anything once, and if it did not kill him, maybe twice.

12 years of Catholic education and a couple of years in college spread between wild drug induce euphoric years, which did not kill him, gave James an unique moral compass that swings in any direction it wants. A scientific mind and a spirit that believes nothing is impossible if you want it bad enough guides his writings. He enjoys traveling to new places and seeing what life has to offer.

James began writing short stories and poetry back in his early years. In his twenties moved on to novels. He worked in the financial industry and later got a degree in computer programming, his other love. James has a successful career as a software engineer designing, developing and maintaining systems for the government and the private sector. He has been programming for nearly forty years in various languages.

After years in the computer world he returned to his first love, unleashing the characters in his head. Still a hopeless insomniac, he feels free to pound out plots. James L Hill is a prolific storyteller writing crime stories, fantasies, and science fiction, with a slant on the dark side of life.

The next step on his journey naturally led to the business of publishing. He started RockHill Publishing LLC not only to produce his own work, but to give others access to the literary world. His computer background and experiences in word processing gives him insight into what it takes to publish good books.

The Killer series is an adult crime novel centered around the life of Bulletproof Morris 'Mojo' Johnson. *Killer With A Heart* introduces us to the young gangsters and mobsters in the conflicting worlds of Organized Crime.

Killer With Three Heads has the boys from the Bronx return as international criminals and more deadly than ever.

The Emerald Lady is a pirate/mermaid adventure/love story set in the Golden Age of Pirate and the first novel in the fantasy Gemstone Series.

Pegasus: A Journey To New Eden, his science fictions deal with the emotional effects of technology, and answers the question, "How do I feel about nuclear war?"

He lives in Virginia Beach has six kids and eleven grandchildren.

If you enjoyed reading this book, please leave
James a review and let him know.

Here are more titles by JL Hill:

Killer With A Heart

Killer With Three Heads

Here are more titles by James L Hill:

The Emerald Lady

RockHill Publishing LLC

There are some lessons that only time can teach, but
you do not learn talent, you only perfect it over time.

www.rockhillpublishing.com